Anonymous

# Regulations

Bureau of the provost Marshal

Anonymous

**Regulations**
*Bureau of the provost Marshal*

ISBN/EAN: 9783337381004

Printed in Europe, USA, Canada, Australia, Japan

Cover: Foto ©Andreas Hilbeck / pixelio.de

More available books at **www.hansebooks.com**

# WAR DEPARTMENT.

---

## REGULATIONS

FOR THE

## GOVERNMENT OF THE BUREAU

OF

# THE PROVOST MARSHAL GENERAL

OF

## THE UNITED STATES.

---

PROVOST-MARSHAL GENERAL'S OFFICE,
*Washington, April* 24, 1863.

---

WASHINGTON:
GOVERNMENT PRINTING OFFICE.
1863.

WAR DEPARTMENT,

*Washington, April* 21, 1863.

The following regulations for the government of the Bureau of the Provost Marshal General of the United States, having been approved by the President of the United States, he commands that they be published for the government of all concerned, and that they be strictly observed.

EDWIN M. STANTON,

*Secretary of War.*

# INDEX.

## A.



## B.

## E.

## N.



## O.



## P.

# REGULATIONS

FOR

THE GOVERNMENT

OF THE

# BUREAU OF THE PROVOST MARSHAL GENERAL

OF

# THE UNITED STATES.

---

## OFFICERS DETAILED AS ACTING ASSISTANT PROVOST MARSHALS GENERAL FOR STATES.

1. The officer detailed in each State to aid the War Department in securing uniformity in the execution of the enrolment act shall keep himself well informed as to the condition of the department throughout the State. He shall, under the provost marshal general of the United States, exercise supervision over the provost marshals and their subordinates for the congressional districts of that State. He shall communicate to them the orders and instructions of the provost marshal general, and see that they are promptly and efficiently executed. He shall from time to time give or transmit such instructions in accordance with these regulations, as hereinafter prescribed, as may be required to facilitate and enforce obedience to them.

2. He shall forward to the provost marshal general, with his remarks, all communications transmitted through his office.

3. He will communicate freely with the governor and other State, town, county, or city officers, and, with their sanction, will extract such information from their records as may facilitate the business of provost marshals and boards of enrolment. He shall communicate this and all other useful information to the provost marshals or boards of enrolment, and shall obtain from them copies of such reports and rolls as may be required for the records of the State authorities.

4. He shall make full and frequent reports to the provost marshal general on the condition and wants of the service in the State; and shall apply to him for instructions regarding all doubtful points in the discharge of his duty.

5. The following is from section 4th of the act for enrolling and calling out the national forces, &c., approved March 3, 1863: "That for greater convenience in enrolling, calling out, and organizing the national forces, and for the arrest of deserters and spies of the enemy, the United States shall be divided into districts, of which the District of Columbia shall constitute one, each Territory of the United States shall constitute one or more, as the President shall direct, and each congressional district of the respective States, as fixed by law of the State next preceding the enrolment, shall constitute one: *Provided,* That in States which have not by their laws been divided into two or more congressional districts, the President of the United States shall divide the same into so many enrolment districts as he may deem fit and convenient."

PROVOST MARSHALS.

6. The following is from section 5th of the act for enrolling and calling out the national forces, &c., approved March 3, 1863: "That for each of said districts there shall be appointed by the President a provost marshal, with the rank, pay, and emoluments of a captain of cavalry, or an officer of said rank shall be detailed by the President, who shall be under the direction and subject to the orders of a provost marshal general, appointed or detailed by the President of the United States, whose office shall be at the seat of government, forming a separate bureau of the War Department, and whose rank, pay, and emoluments shall be those of a colonel of cavalry."

DISTRICT HEADQUARTERS.

7. The headquarters of each district shall be fixed and announced by the provost marshal general.

8. Each provost marshal shall take post at the headquarters of his district.

9. Each provost marshal, on taking post, shall, if there be no government building suitable for the purpose, make, subject to approval, written agreement for the rent of an office, upon the most reasonable terms possible; and two copies of this contract shall be forwarded immediately to the provost marshal general. This office will consist of not more than three rooms; one of which shall be used by the board of enrolment during its sessions, and may be devoted at other times to the wants of the service. The rent will be paid as hereinafter provided for other accounts.

10. Each provost marshal may employ two clerks, subject to the approval of the provost marshal general, and at a rate of compensation to be fixed by him. One of these clerks shall, in addition to his other duties, act as recorder of the board of enrolment; and both may be appointed deputy provost marshals for local purposes, but shall not be entitled to additional compensation therefor. Provost marshals, in reporting the appointments of their clerks, will send to the provost marshal general a specimen of the handwriting of each one appointed, and shall recommend the amount of compensation proper to be allowed him.

### DEPUTY PROVOST MARSHALS AND AGENTS.

11. Two deputy provost marshals for each district composed of more than one county may be appointed, subject to the approval of the provost marshal general; and if more are thought to be necessary, the number required, the places where, and the reasons why, with all the facts, will be reported through the acting assistant provost marshal general for the State, with such recommendations in each case as may be deemed pertinent. The pay of a deputy provost marshal shall not be more than $100 per month.

12. Special officers or agents, for detecting and arresting deserters and spies, may be employed when necessary, but not more than four shall be employed in a district without the approval of the provost marshal general. They may be paid at the rate of forty (40) to sixty-five (65) dollars per month, depending on their usefulness.

### DUTIES OF PROVOST MARSHALS.

13. Immediately upon entering upon his duties, each provost marshal shall report by letter to the provost marshal general of the United States and the acting assistant provost marshal general for his State. In case no such acting assistant provost marshal general has been assigned, he will place himself at once in communication with the governor of the State.

14. He will place himself in communication with the principal executive officers of the civil service within his district, and all officers commanding organized military forces therein. He shall also acquaint himself with the approximate strength of these forces, and the regular stations occupied by them.

15. He shall see to securing and rendering the vouchers and accounts incident to all services pertaining to his office.

16. Section 7th, act for enrolling and calling out the national forces, approved March 3, 1863, is as follows: "*And be it further enacted,* That it shall be the duty of the provost marshals to arrest all deserters, whether regulars, volunteers, militiamen, or persons called into the service under this or any other act of Congress, wherever they may be found, and to send them to the nearest military commander or military post; to detect, seize, and confine spies of the enemy, who shall, without unreasonable delay, be delivered to the custody of the general commanding the department in which they may be arrested, to be tried as soon as the exigencies of the service permit; to obey all lawful orders and regulations of the provost marshal general, and such as may be prescribed by law, concerning the enrolment and calling into service of the national forces."

17. When transportation is required by the provost marshal for deserters after their arrest, or for the military guards in charge of them, he shall make requisition for it on the United States quartermaster, if there be one accessible; if not, he shall procure transportation and take vouchers as hereinafter provided.

18. It shall be the duty of the provost marshal in each district to call together, whenever required, the board of enrolment; to preside at its sessions,

announce such of its decisions or directions as it may be necessary to make public, enforce its orders, see that a fair record is made of its proceedings in a book kept for that purpose by the recorder, and to transmit to the provost marshal general the enrolment lists, as consolidated by the board, and such other communications as the board may deem it necessary to lay before the provost marshal general.

19. The provost marshal shall himself, or through his deputies, carry out that part of section 12th of the enrolment act which requires that the persons drawn in the draft "shall be notified of the same within ten days thereafter, by a written or printed notice, to be served personally, or by leaving a copy, at the last place of residence, requiring them to appear at a designated rendezvous to report for duty." And all persons so drawn in the draft shall report at the place of rendezvous on the day required by said notice, which shall be within ten days after such notice has been thus served upon them.

20. He shall file with the district attorney of the United States, for the district in which the offence shall have been committed, written information, containing a report of the facts against any and all persons within his district who shall have violated section 24th of the enrolment act, or any part of the same, which section is in the following terms, to wit:

"SEC. 24. *And be it further enacted*, That every person not subject to the rules and articles of war who shall procure or entice, or attempt to procure or entice, a soldier in the service of the United States to desert; or who shall harbor, conceal, or give employment to a deserter, or carry him away, or aid in carrying him away, knowing him to be such; or who shall purchase from any soldier his arms, equipments, ammunition, uniform, clothing, or any part thereof; and any captain or commanding officer of any ship or vessel, or any superintendent or conductor of any railroad, or any other public conveyance, carrying away any such soldier as one of his crew or otherwise, knowing him to have deserted, or shall refuse to deliver him up to the orders of his commanding officer, shall, upon legal conviction, be fined, at the discretion of any court having cognizance of the same, in any sum not exceeding five hundred dollars, and he shall be imprisoned not exceeding two years nor less than six months."

21. He shall arrest and forthwith deliver to the proper civil authorities, to wit, the marshal of the United States within and for the district in which the arrest is made, with written charges in the case, any and all persons who, shall have violated section 25th of the enrolment act, or any part of the same, which section is in the following terms, to wit:

"SEC. 25. *And be it further enacted*, That if any person shall resist any draft of men enrolled under this act into the service of the United States, or shall counsel or aid any person to resist any such draft, or shall assault or obstruct any officer in making such draft, or in the performance of any service in relation thereto, or shall counsel any person to assault or obstruct any such officer, or shall counsel any drafted men not to appear at the place of rendezvous, or wilfully dissuade them from the performance of military duty as required by law, such person shall be subject to summary arrest by the provost marshal, and shall be forthwith delivered to the civil authorities, and, upon conviction thereof, be punished by a fine not exceeding five hundred dollars, or by imprisonment not exceeding two years, or by both of said punishments."

Provost marshals are required to execute this duty with firmness, but with prudence and good judgment, and without unnecessary harshness.

22. It shall be the duty of the provost marshal to prepare and forward, through the assistant provost marshal general for his State, to the provost marshal general, charges and specifications in due form against the surgeon of the board of enrolment in his district, if said surgeon omits any of the duties, or renders himself liable to any of the penalties set forth in sections 14th and 15th of the enrolment act, which are in the following terms, to wit:

"Sec. 14. *And be it further enacted,* That all drafted persons shall, on arriving at the rendezvous, be carefully inspected by the surgeon of the board, who shall truly report to the board the physical condition of each one; and all persons drafted and claiming exemption from military duty on account of disability, or any other cause, shall present their claims to be exempted to the board, whose decision shall be final."

"Sec. 15. *And be it further enacted,* That any surgeon charged with the duty of such inspection who shall receive from any person whomsoever any money or other valuable thing, or agree, directly or indirectly, to receive the same to his own or another's use, for making an imperfect inspection or a false or incorrect report, or who shall wilfully neglect to make a faithful inspection and true report, shall be tried by a court-martial, and, on conviction thereof, be punished by fine not exceeding five hundred dollars nor less than two hundred, and be imprisoned at the discretion of the court, and be cashiered and dismissed from the service."

23. The provost marshal shall, so far as it may be in his power, make the seizures provided for in section 23d of the enrolment act, which section is in the following terms, to wit:

"Sec. 23. *And be it further enacted,* That the clothes, arms, military outfits, and accoutrements furnished by the United States to any soldier shall not be sold, bartered, exchanged, pledged, loaned, or given away; and no person not a soldier, or duly authorized officer of the United States, who has possession of any such clothes, arms, military outfits, or accoutrements, furnished as aforesaid, and which have been the subjects of any such sale, barter, exchange, pledge, loan, or gift, shall have any right, title, or interest therein; but the same may be seized and taken wherever found by any officer of the United States, civil or military, and shall thereupon be delivered to any quartermaster or other officer authorized to receive the same; and the possession of any such clothes, arms, military outfits, or accoutrements, by any person not a soldier or officer of the United States, shall be *prima facie* evidence of such a sale, barter, exchange, pledge, loan, or gift, as aforesaid."

24. Provost marshals are expected and required to complete all business which may originate in or properly belong to their respective districts, though

in doing so, they or their deputies or agents may, for the time, be carried within the geographical limits of other districts.

25. To enable provost marshals to discharge their duties efficiently, they are authorized to call upon the nearest available military force, or on citizens as a *posse comitatus*, or on United States marshals and deputy marshals; and these and all other persons are hereby enjoined to aid the provost marshal in the execution of his lawful duties when called on so to do.

26. Provost marshals will report, from time to time, as to what they deem necessary to secure an efficient performance of the duties required of them, and a complete execution of the law under which they act, giving the names and object of employés proposed.

27. Each provost marshal shall conform to the special instructions hereinafter set forth, and communicate promptly and fully, through the acting assistant provost marshal general for his State, such information and suggestions as he may deem of importance.

### APPREHENSION AND DELIVERY OF DESERTERS.

28. Every possible effort must be made by the provost marshal to secure the arrest of all deserters within his district; he shall see that they are properly held after arrest, and that all deserters arrested by other parties and presented to him, or at his headquarters, are promptly received and held in secure custody until delivered at the nearest military station.

29. The five dollars reward authorized by law for the delivery of a deserter is, of course, only due in case the man presented is actually a deserter. It is, however, ordered that the provost marshal shall decide whether the reward shall be paid or withheld; and he is directed to permit as little delay as possible in making this decision, in order that persons who bring deserters may receive the reward surely and *promptly*.

30. Provost marshals or deputy provost marshals are not entitled to receive the reward for the apprehension of deserters.

31. Provost marshals shall keep books in which they shall enter the description of all deserters and other persons received as prisoners by them, with such dates and remarks, as may be proper to complete, as far as practicable, the history of the arrest and of the man. They shall also keep such other books as may be necessary to preserve a complete history of their correspondence and business.

32. Where there is a military station in the immediate vicinity of the headquarters of the district, the provost marshal will send the deserters to it on the day of, or day following their arrest by, or delivery to, him. Where, however, the district headquarters are remote from all military stations, the deserters will be sent tri-monthly, or oftener if there be more than five on hand at any intermediate period.

33. When it is necessary to conduct and guard deserters from district headquarters to a military station, and there be no military force available for

this service, the provost marshal may employ a suitable special guard, under a deputy, to accompany the prisoners. The members of the guard may be allowed, for the time actually and necessarily employed in the trip, a per diem of not more than $1, besides their actual expenses, provided they accomplish the duty assigned them.

34. The provost marshal shall see that the guards, sent from his district to the military station in charge of deserters, are armed, and instructed to prevent the escape of those in their custody.

35. The district provost marshal shall see that descriptive lists, *in duplicate*, are made of every deserter, or party of deserters, sent off by him. These lists will be taken by the provost marshal or deputy in charge of the deserters to the officer to whom the deserters are turned over; this latter officer will retain one, and return the other, giving a receipt for the deserters, by name, on the back of it; this copy of the descriptive list will accompany the provost marshal's monthly report to the provost marshal general of persons arrested. The expenses incurred in the apprehension of deserters, and the five dollars paid as reward, if this sum has been justly claimed and a voucher given by the provost marshal for it, will be stated opposite each man's name on the descriptive lists, None of the expenses, however, incurred on the deserter's account after he has been received by the provost marshal shall be charged against him.

36. By section 13th of the enrolment act, any person failing to report after due service of notice, as prescribed in the act, without furnishing a substitute, or paying the requisite sum therefor, shall be deemed a deserter, and shall be arrested by the provost marshal and sent to the nearest military post for trial by court-martial, unless, upon proper showing that he is not liable to do military duty, the board of enrolment shall relieve him from draft. In case of such arrests, the provost marshal shall send with each deserter to the military post written charges against him.

37. Provost marshals, while enjoined to a strict and inflexible performance of duty, are warned against improper arrests. It may happen that discharged soldiers may be imposed upon and deprived of their papers, and then delivered, for reward, to the provost marshal as deserters. Sagacity and prompt and close scrutiny of every case, on the part of provost marshals, must be exercised to prevent abuse or hardship of this nature.

## SPIES.

38. It is the duty of provost marshals "to detect, seize, and confine spies of the enemy who shall, without unreasonable delay, be delivered to the custody of the general commanding the department in which they may be arrested."

39. Spies, when arrested, must be securely guarded and conducted to the custody of the *general commanding the department*, by military or special guards, in a manner similar to that heretofore provided for deserters.

40. The accounts for all expenses in regard to the arrest, confinement, trans-

portation, and subsistence of spies will be similar to those prescribed for deserters. The fact of their being rendered in relation to a spy and not to a deserter must be stated.

RESTS.—QUARTERING AND SUBSISTING PROVOST MARSHALS' PARTIES.

41. Written agreements will be made by provost marshals for the rent of "rests," upon the most reasonable terms possible, subject to approval; and two copies of this contract forwarded immediately to the provost marshal general. The rent will be paid as hereinafter directed for other accounts.

42. Where district headquarters are in cities, or elsewhere, within reach of any of the regular posts, encampments, "Soldiers' Rests," or other places of accommodation provided by the government, or by the public, for soldiers, the provost marshal shall make it his duty to avail himself of them in providing for deserters, stragglers, &c.; and when moving deserters or other men under his control from one point to another, he shall seek and avail himself of these places of accommodation. If there be no such places of accommodation within convenient reach of district headquarters, the provost marshal shall at once establish a "rest," by written agreement with some responsible party, to provide cooked rations, on demand, for as many soldiers as he may, from time to time, present, and at a rate not to exceed thirty cents a day for each person actually subsisted.

43. After deserters are received by the provost marshal, they and the guards in charge of them must be subsisted at the "rest" or station as heretofore provided.

44. When subsistence cannot be issued by the commissariat to the provost marshals' parties, it will be procured by the provost marshal on written contracts, when practicable, for complete rations. If the ration cannot be procured thus, then a contract will be made for board and lodging. The aggregate cost of board and lodging should never exceed forty cents per diem; as a general rule, experience has indicated that it should be much less.

45. Accounts for subsistence of persons in the military service will be kept distinct from those for citizens, such as citizen employés of the provost marshal's department, spies, or others not officers or soldiers in United States service.

46. The contractor will send for payment monthly or quarterly, at his option, his accounts for rations issued to persons in military service, to the commissary general; and for citizens and drafted men while at the rendezvous, to the provost marshal general.

47. When convenience and economy require that the contract shall be for board and lodging, the contract shall state the amount for each separately. The contractor will be paid for board as prescribed in the preceding paragraph; and for lodging from the provost marshal general's funds as hereinafter directed.

48. When a contract cannot be made, the provost marshal may make arrangements for the payment of the necessary expenses of subsisting and boarding his party.

49. When issues of rations are made in kind, it will be done on the usual provision returns. Board will be furnished on a return, showing the number of the party, the days and dates.

50. Lodging will be furnished on a return, showing the number of men, days, and dates for each. From these returns the abstract is made up.—(Form 19.)

51. Where "rests" have not been established, and no place of security is at hand, prisoners in charge of provost marshals' parties may be quartered in jails. In such cases the ordinary jail-fees will be paid in lieu of board and lodging. (See paragraph 118.)

52. When prisoners are to be sent from a station to their destination, as provided in section 7 of the enrolment act of March 3, 1863, they and their guards will be supplied, before leaving the station, with cooked provisions for the trip.

53. Upon their return, or when travelling on duty, the guards must, when practicable, avail themselves of the "rests" or stations on the route.

### BOARDS OF ENROLMENT.

54. Section 8th of act for enrolling and calling out the national forces, &c., approved March 3, 1863, provides "That in each of said districts there shall be a board of enrolment, to be composed of the provost marshal as president, and two other persons, to be appointed by the President of the United States, one of whom shall be a licensed and practicing physician and surgeon."

55. Section 5th of act making appropriations for sundry civil expenses of the government for the year ending June 30, 1864, and for the year ending June 30, 1863, and for other purposes, approved March 3, 1863, provides "That the surgeon and the citizen at large, who are, with the provost marshal, to form the enrolling board of each congressional district, shall receive the compensation of an assistant surgeon of the army, excluding commutation for fuel and quarters for the time actually employed, and that the same may be paid by the Secretary of War out of appropriations already made for the services of that department." Payment shall be made to them and to the provost marshal by the pay department.

### DUTIES OF BOARDS OF ENROLMENT.

56. Section 9th of act for enrolling and calling out the national forces, &c., approved March 3, 1863, provides "That it shall be the duty of the said board to divide the district into sub-districts of convenient size, if they shall deem it necessary, not exceeding two, without the direction of the Secretary of War, and to appoint, on or before the 10th day of March next, and in each alternate year thereafter, an enrolling officer for each sub-district, and to furnish him with proper blanks and instructions; and he shall immediately proceed to enroll all persons subject to military duty, noting their respective places of residence, ages on the first day of July following, and their occupation, and

shall, on or before the first day of April, report the same to the board of enrolment, to be consolidated into one list, a copy of which shall be transmitted to the provost marshal general, on or before the first day of May succeeding the enrolment: *Provided, nevertheless,* That if, from any cause, the duties prescribed by this section cannot be performed within the time specified, then the same shall be performed as soon thereafter as practicable."

57. To carry out the provisions of the foregoing act, and for the purpose of enrolment, the board in each district is hereby directed by the Secretary of War to divide each district, whenever the board shall deem it expedient, into sub-districts at the rate of one for each ward of a city; and if the board deem it best, one or more townships of a county may constitute a sub-district, where the population is dense, or a county may be made a sub-district in sparsely settled regions. The object to be kept in view by the board shall be to make such subdivisions as to insure the completion of the enrolment at the earliest date practicable.

58. The board shall, by its majority, appoint, with the least practicable delay, an enrolling officer for each sub-district, and shall take pains to see that fit and proper persons are selected for this duty. Assessors, if otherwise suitable, are preferable for this position. The enrolling officers may be paid not to exceed three dollars per diem for the time actually employed.

59. The board will give the enrolling officers all necessary instructions, as they act under its direction.

60. The board shall require of each enrolling officer, before he enters on his duties, an oath duly administered and witnessed, that he will perform faithfully, and without partiality, favor, or affection, all the duties of his office as enrolling officer of the sub-district to which he is appointed, and that he will obey all lawful instructions of the board of enrolment.

61. The enrolling officer for each district or sub-district shall, immediately upon his appointment, proceed to enroll all persons subject to military duty under the provisions of the act for enrolling and calling out the national forces. He shall note their respective places of residence, their ages, as they will be upon the 1st day of July, 1863, their color, whether white or black, and their occupations, respectively.

62. This enrolment must include:

1. All able-bodied male citizens of the United States, between the ages of twenty and forty-five years, not exempt from military service by law.
2. All persons of foreign birth, not so exempted, who shall have declared, on oath, their intention to become citizens of the United States under and in pursuance of the laws thereof.

63. Section 3d of act for enrolling and calling out the national forces, &c., approved March 3, 1863, provides "That the national forces of the United States not now in the military service, enrolled under this act, shall be divided into two classes: the first of which shall comprise all persons subject to do military

duty between the ages of twenty and thirty-five years, and all unmarried persons subject to do military duty above the age of thirty-five and under the age of forty-five; the second class shall comprise all other persons subject to do military duty; and they shall not, in any district, be called into the service of the United States until those of the first class shall have been called."

64. The enrolment of each class shall be made separately, on sheets by itself, (Forms 35 and 36;) but the enrolment of both classes shall be carried on at the same time.

65. Persons having their legal domicile within any district are not exempt from enrolment therein by reason of temporary absence therefrom. Students in colleges or schools, teachers, apprentices, sailors, travellers, travelling merchants and similar classes of citizens, must be enrolled in the districts in which they have their respective domiciles.

66. The board shall require the enrolling officers to judge of the ages of individuals by the best information they can obtain in each case, but always to make a decision as to whether the person in question is subject to enrolment, and if so, in which class, and to enroll him accordingly. The board will decide questions of exemption on account of age, when brought before it, under the law, by the persons enrolled.

67. In city districts the board shall require the enrolling officers to submit their lists, as far as completed, daily or every other day; and if the district is composed of a county, the lists shall be required twice a week, or weekly if the board deem it best. As soon as these partial lists are received by the board, they must be entered on the copy for the provost marshal general, *alphabetically arranged.*

68. As soon as the enrolment is completed in each district, the consolidated list for the provost marshal general, with the names alphabetically arranged, must be completed and forwarded direct to him with the least possible delay.

69. The board shall preserve the rolls of the enrolment sub-districts; and on the consolidated lists for the provost marshal general, a recapitulation shall be made in figures, (according to form,) showing the number of men, whether white or colored, of each class enrolled in each ward or township, and the total number of each class enrolled in the district.

70. Where complete enrolments have been lately made by State authority, copies thereof will be obtained, if practicable, and used in making or verifying the new enrolments.

71. Whenever any part of the national forces in a district is to be called out, the number of men to come from each district will be announced to the board, through the provost marshal general, with specific instructions as to the sub-divisions to be considered for the district with a view to making the apportionment.

72. The board shall make the apportionment according to the sub-districts to be considered, and shall then make the draft for each sub-district of the number of men required, and fifty per cent. in addition.

73. The board shall make an exact and complete roll of the names of the persons drafted, and of the order in which they were drawn, so that the first drawn may stand first on the said roll, and the second may stand second, and so on. The draft shall take place at the headquarters of the district. It shall be public, and under the direction of the board of enrolment. The name of each person enrolled shall be placed in a box to be provided for the purpose, and the provost marshal, or some person designated by him, (the drawer to be blindfolded,) shall draw therefrom one name at a time until the required number is obtained.

74. The exact and complete roll of the names of persons drawn in the draft shall be entered by the board in a book to be kept for that purpose, ruled and headed to correspond with the descriptive roll of drafted men.—(Form 34.)

75. The number required to fill the call will be taken from this roll, by commencing at the first name, and taking in order, until the required number is obtained, all who are not, by the board, decided to be excepted and exempt under the provisions of the enrolment act.

76. The names of the men, thus called into service, will be entered on "descriptive rolls," (in triplicate,) signed by the board. One copy of this roll will be sent to the provost marshal general direct, one copy to the acting assistant provost marshal general of the State, and one will be retained by the provost marshal.

77. Certified extracts from this descriptive roll shall be made in duplicate by the provost marshal for every party of drafted men sent off, and sent with the party to the officer to whom the party is to be delivered. One copy is to be retained by this officer, and the other is to be returned, with a receipt for the party as delivered to him on the back. The returned copy will accompany the provost marshal's monthly report to the provost marshal general.

78. The board shall note on the roll-book of drafted men, in the column of remarks opposite each man's name, the disposition made of him—whether called into service and sent to the rendezvous, exempted by the board, replaced by a substitute, commuted for, deserted, or discharged as not being required.

79. The substitute whom any drafted person is authorized, by section 13th of the enrolment act, to furnish, must be presented to the board of enrolment; and it shall be the duty of the board to examine him, and, if accepted, to place his name on the book of persons drafted, with explanatory remarks. His name will then be transcribed on the descriptive rolls of men called into service.

80. Certificates of exemption from the draft, by reason of having provided a substitute, or having paid commutation money, shall be furnished by the board of enrolment according to form 31. A discharge from one draft furnishes no exemption from any subsequent draft, except that when the person drafted has furnished an acceptable substitute, and has received a certificate of discharge from a preceding draft, he shall be held exempt from military duty during the time for which he had been drafted and for which such substitute was furnished.

81. The board shall furnish a discharge (Form 31) from further liabilities under the particular draft, to any drafted person who presents a *bona fide* receipt,

for the sum announced in orders for the procuration of substitutes, from the person authorized by the Secretary of War to receive it.

82. All persons exempted from the draft by the board (section 14, enrolment act,) shall be furnished with certificate of the fact, (Form 32,) and all persons "discharged," after the required number of able-bodied men shall have been obtained, shall be furnished by the board with a certificate.—(Form 33.)

83. The character and amount of evidence requisite to decide the question of disqualification on account of age must be determined by the board of enrolment. Such disqualification should be clearly and fully proved to the board, before exemption is granted under this plea. The following rules should be carefully regarded, viz:

The affidavit of the person claiming exemption must, in all cases, be required, supported by as much of the following testimony as can be obtained, or may be deemed requisite:

1. By an authenticated extract from the legal registry of births if there be any such registry.
2. By any other authenticated documentary evidence tending to establish the fact of age.
3. By the affidavit of the parents.
4. By the affidavits of such other respectable persons, (not less than two,) heads of families, as are most likely to be informed on the subject.

The amount of evidence herein required to establish a claim to exemption is the least which the board should accept; and if in any case the board has reason to doubt the character or sufficiency of the evidence presented, it should decline granting the exemption, unless such additional proof as it may require be produced in time to be considered, without delaying the business of the draft.

### EXEMPTIONS, AND RULES OF EVIDENCE, BY WHICH THEY ARE TO BE DETERMINED.

84. Section 2, act for enrolling and calling out the national forces, &c., approved March 3, 1863, provides as follows: "That the following persons be, and they are hereby, excepted and exempt from the provisions of this act, and shall not be liable to military duty under the same, to wit: Such as are rejected as physically or mentally unfit for the service; also, first, the Vice-President of the United States, the judges of the various courts of the United States, the heads of the various executive departments of the government, and the governors of the several States. Second, the only son liable to military duty, of a widow dependent upon his labor for support. Third, the only son of aged or infirm parent or parents dependent upon his labor for support. Fourth, where there are two or more sons of aged or infirm parents subject to draft, the father, or, if he be dead, the mother, may elect which son shall be exempt. Fifth, the only brother of children not twelve years old, having neither father nor mother, dependent upon his labor for support. Sixth, the father of motherless children under twelve years of age, dependent upon his labor for support.

Seventh, where there are a father and sons in the same family and household, and two of them are in the military service of the United States as non-commissioned officers, musicians, or privates, the residue of such family and household, not exceeding two, shall be exempt. And no persons but such as are herein excepted shall be exempt: *Provided, however,* That no person who has been convicted of any felony shall be enrolled or permitted to serve in said forces."

85. The following diseases and infirmities are those which disqualify for military service, and for which only, drafted men are to be "rejected as physically or mentally unfit for the service," viz:

1. Manifest imbecility or insanity.
2. Epilepsy. For this disability the statement of the drafted man is insufficient, and the fact must be established by the duly attested affidavit of a physician, of good standing, who has attended him in a convulsion.
3. Paralysis, general or of one limb, or chorea; their existence to be adequately determined.
4. Acute or organic diseases of the brain or spinal chord; of the heart or lungs; of the stomach or intestines; of the liver or spleen; of the kidneys or bladder, sufficient to have impaired the general health, or so well marked as to leave no reasonable doubt of the man's incapacity for military service.
5. Confirmed consumption; cancer; aneurism of the large arteries.
6. Inveterate and extensive disease of the skin, which will necessarily impair his efficiency as a soldier.
7. Decided feebleness of constitution, whether natural or acquired.
8. Scrofula or constitutional syphilis, which has resisted treatment and seriously impaired his general health.
9. Habitual and confirmed intemperance or solitary vice, in degree sufficient to have materially enfeebled the constitution.
10. Chronic rheumatism, unless manifested by positive change of structure, wasting of the affected limb, or puffiness or distortion of the joints, does not exempt. Impaired motion of joints and contraction of the limbs alleged to arise from rheumatism, and in which the nutrition of the limb is not manifestly impaired, are to be proved by examination while in a state of anaesthesia induced by ether only.
11. Pain, whether simulating headache, neuralgia in any of its forms, rheumatism, lumbago, or affections of the muscles, bones, or joints, is a symptom of disease so easily pretended that it is not to be admitted as a cause for exemption unless accompanied with manifest derangement of the general health, wasting of a limb, or other positive sign of disqualifying local disease.
12. Great injuries or diseases of the skull, occasioning impairment of the intellectual faculties, epilepsy, or other manifest nervous or spasmodic symptoms.

13. Total loss of sight; loss of sight of right eye; cataract; loss of crystalline lens of right eye.
14. Other serious diseases of the eye affecting its integrity and use, *e. g.:* chronic ophthalmia, fistula lachrymalis, ptosis, (if real,) ectropion, entropion, &c. Myopia, unless very decided or depending upon some structural change in the eye, is not a cause for exemption.
15. Loss of nose; deformity of nose so great as seriously to obstruct respiration; ozæna, dependent upon caries in progress.
16. Complete deafness. This disability must not be admitted on the mere statement of the drafted man, but must be proved by the existence of positive disease, or by other satisfactory evidence. Purulent otorrhœa.
17. Caries of the superior or inferior maxilla, of the nasal or palate bones, if in progress; cleft palate, (bony;) extensive loss of substance of the cheeks, or salivary fistula.
18. Dumbness; permanent loss of voice; not to be admitted without clear and satisfactory proof.
19. Total loss of tongue; mutilation or partial loss of tongue, provided the mutilation be extensive enough to interfere with the necessary use of the organ.
20. Hypertrophy or atrophy of the tongue, sufficient in degree to impair speech or deglutition; obstinate chronic ulceration of the tongue.
21. Stammering, if excessive and confirmed; to be established by satisfactory evidence, under oath.
22. Loss of a sufficient number of teeth to prevent proper mastication of food and tearing the cartridge.
23. Incurable deformities or loss of part of either jaw, hindering biting of the cartridge or proper mastication, or greatly injuring speech; anchylosis of lower jaw.
24. Tumors of the neck, impeding respiration or deglutition; fistula of larynx or trachea; torticollis, if of long standing and well marked.
25. Deformity of the chest sufficient to impede respiration, or to prevent the carrying of arms and military equipments; caries of the ribs.
26. Deficient amplitude and power of expansion of chest. A man five feet three inches (minimum standard height for the regular army,) should not measure less than thirty inches in circumference immediately above the nipples, and have an expansive mobility of not less than two inches.
27. Abdomen grossly protuberant; excessive obesity; hernia, either inguinal or femoral.
28. Artificial anus; stricture of the rectum; prolapsus ani. Fistula in ano is not a positive disqualification, but may be so, if extensive or complicated with visceral disease.
29. Old and ulcerated internal hæmorrhoids, if in degree sufficient to

impair the man's efficiency. External hæmorrhoids are no cause for exemption.

30. Total loss or nearly total loss of penis; epispadia or hypospadia at the middle or near the root of the penis.
31. Incurable permanent organic stricture of the urethra, in which the urine is passed drop by drop, or which is complicated by disease of the bladder; urinary fistula. Recent or spasmodic stricture of the urethra, does not exempt.
32. Incontinence of urine, being a disease frequently feigned and of rare occurrence, is not, of itself, a cause for exemption. Stone in the bladder, ascertained by the introduction of the metallic catheter, is a positive disqualification.
33. Loss or complete atrophy of both testicles from any cause; permanent retention of one or both testicles within the inguinal canal; but voluntary retraction does not exempt.
34. Confirmed or malignant sarcocele; hydrocele, if complicated with organic disease of the testicle. Varicocele and cirsocele are not, in themselves, disqualifying.
35. Excessive anterior or posterior curvature of the spine; caries of the spine.
36. Loss of an arm, forearm, hand, thigh, leg, or foot.
37. Wounds, fractures, tumors, atrophy of a limb, or chronic diseases of the joints or bones, that would impede marching or prevent continuous muscular exertion.
38. Anchylosis or irreducible dislocation of the shoulder, elbow, wrist, hip, knee, or ankle joint.
39. Muscular or cutaneous contractions from wounds or burns, in degree sufficient to prevent useful motion of a limb.
40. Total loss of a thumb; loss of ungual phalanx of right thumb.
41. Total loss of any two fingers of same hand.
42. Total loss of index finger of right hand.
43. Loss of the first and second phalanges of the fingers of right hand.
44. Permanent extension or permanent contraction of any finger except the little finger; all the fingers adherent or united.
45. Total loss of either great toe; loss of any three toes on the same foot; all the toes joined together.
46. The great toe crossing the other toes with great prominence of the articulation of the metatarsal bone and first phalanx of the great toe.
47. Overriding or superposition of all the toes.
48. Permanent retraction of the last phalanx of one of the toes, so that the free border of the nail bears upon the ground; or flexion at a right angle of the first phalanx of a toe upon a second, with anchylosis of this articulation.
49. Club feet; splay feet, where the arch is so far effaced that the tuber-

osity of the scaphoid bone touches the ground and the line of station runs along the whole internal border of the foot, with great prominence of the inner ankle; but ordinary, large, ill-shaped or flat feet do not exempt.

50. Varicose veins of inferior extremities, if large and numerous, having clusters of knots, and accompanied with chronic swellings or ulcerations.

51. Chronic ulcers; extensive, deep, and adherent cicatrices of lower extremities.

86. No certificate of a physician or surgeon is to be received in support of any point in the claim of drafted men for exemption from military service, unless the facts and statements therein set forth are affirmed or sworn to before a civil magistrate competent to administer oaths.

87. The exempts under the first provision of section 2 of the act for enrolling and calling out the national forces, &c., will generally be sufficiently well known to the board to obviate the necessity of evidence with regard to them. Should, however, the board consider it necessary, in any case, the commission or certificate of office of any person claiming exemption under the provision mentioned may be required to be shown.

88. To establish exemption under the second, third, fourth, fifth, and sixth provisions of section 2 of the act for enrolling and calling out the national forces, &c., the board shall require the affidavits of the person seeking to be exempt and of two respectable men, (heads of families,) residing in the district, that the man in question is "*the only son liable to military duty of a widow dependent on his labor for support,*" "*the only son of aged or infirm parent or parents dependent on his labor for support,*" or otherwise, according to the particular provision of the section under which the exemption is claimed. These affidavits will be made according to the forms hereinafter prescribed, and must in all cases be taken before a civil magistrate duly authorized to administer oaths. These forms of affidavits shall be published by the board of enrolment in the newspapers of the district, for the information of the public, when a draft is ordered.

89. When a claim for exemption is made under the seventh provision of section 2 of the act for enrolling and calling out the national forces, &c., the board shall apply to the provost marshal general for the necessary extracts from the official rolls in the War Department, upon which it shall decide the case.

90. Persons claiming exemption from enrolment must furnish clear proof of their right to such exemption. They will be enrolled where the proof of their exemption is not clear and conclusive.

## INSTRUCTIONS FOR THE PHYSICAL EXAMINATION OF DRAFTED MEN AND SUBSTITUTES.

91. The duty of inspecting men, and of determining whether they are fit or unfit for the military service of the country, requires the utmost impartiality,

skill, and circumspection on the part of the examining surgeon and board of enrolment; for upon the manner in which this duty is performed will depend, in a very great degree, the efficiency of the army.

92. In the examination, the examining surgeons will bear in mind that the object of the government is to secure the services of men who are effective, able-bodied, sober and free from disqualifying diseases.

93. The examining surgeons will also remember that the object of the drafted men, in claiming exemption, may be to escape from service by pretended, simulated, or factitious diseases, or by exaggerating or aggravating those that really exist, and that the design of substitutes frequently is to conceal disqualifying infirmities.

94. The examination by the examining surgeon is to be conducted in the daytime, in the presence of the board of enrolment, and in a room well lighted and sufficiently large for the drafted man to walk about and exercise his limbs, which he must be required to do briskly.

95. The man is to be examined stripped.

96. The surgeon will habitually conduct his examination of a man in the following order, to ascertain:—

1. Whether his limbs are well formed and sufficiently muscular; whether they are ulcerated or extensively cicatrized; whether he has free motion of all his joints, and whether there are any varicose veins, tumors, wounds, fractures, dislocations, or sprains that would impede his marching, or prevent continuous muscular exertion.
2. Whether the thumbs and fingers are complete in number, are well formed, and their motion unimpaired.
3. Whether the feet are sufficiently arched to prevent the tuberosity of the scaphoid bone from touching the ground; whether the toes are complete in number, do not overlap, are not joined together, and whether the great toes are free from bunions.
4. Whether he has any inveterate and extensive disease of the skin.
5. Whether he is sufficiently intelligent; is not subject to convulsions, and whether he has received any contusion or wound of the head that may impair his faculties.
6. Whether his hearing, vision, and speech are good, and whether the eye and its appendages are free from disqualifying diseases.
7. Whether he has a sufficient number of teeth in good condition to masticate his food properly, and to tear his cartridge quickly and with ease. The cartridge is torn with the incisor, canine, or bicuspid teeth.
8. Whether his chest is ample and well formed, in due proportion to his height, and with power of full expansion.
9. Whether there is any structural or serious functional disease of the heart.
10. Whether the abdomen is well formed and not too protuberant; whether either the liver or spleen is considerably enlarged, and whether the rectum and anus are free from disqualifying diseases.

11. Whether the spermatic chords and testes are free from diseases which would impair his efficiency; whether the testes are within the scrotum, and whether he has any rupture.
12. Whether there is any organic disease of the kidney or bladder, or permanent stricture of the urethra.
13. Whether his physical development is good, and constitution neither naturally feeble, nor impaired by disease, habitual intemperance, or solitary vice; whether he is free from phthisis, scrofula, and constitutional syphilis, and whether he is epileptic, imbecile, or insane.

Many of the physical defects above mentioned are insufficient in themselves to disqualify for military service. In determining whether the man is fit or unfit for service, the board must be governed by the list of diseases and infirmities enumerated in paragraph 85.

ACCOUNTS, REPORTS, AND RETURNS.

97. The following are the accounts, reports, and returns to be rendered by provost marshals to the provost marshal general:

1. *Tri-monthly reports* of persons arrested, showing the disposition made of them.—(Form 1.) A copy of this report will be sent to the acting assistant provost marshal general of the State.
2. *Tri-monthly reports* of deserters arrested, stating how disposed of.—(Form 2.) A copy to be sent to the acting assistant provost marshal general of the State.
3. *Tri-monthly reports* of their business and general transactions, in the form of a letter, subdivided into subjects.—(Triplicates.) A copy to be sent to the acting assistant provost marshal general of the State.
4. *Monthly abstract* of indebtedness incurred, (Form 3,) with separate vouchers for each account.
5. *Monthly reports* of persons and articles hired and employed.—(Form 4.) A copy to be sent to the acting assistant provost marshal general of the State.
6. *Monthly reports* of persons arrested, being a consolidation of the tri-monthly reports on the same subject.—(Form 5.) A copy to be sent to the acting assistant provost marshal general of the State.
7. *Monthly returns* of provost marshals' parties and deserters.—(Form 6.) A copy to be sent to the acting assistant provost marshal general of the State.
8. *Monthly returns* of public property.—(Form 7.) An abstract (Form 8) will be made of all the articles purchased during the month. Articles expended, lost, destroyed, &c., to be accounted for on an abstract (Form 9) with vouchers.—(Form 10.)

98. One copy of the monthly reports, returns, &c., must be transmitted to the provost marshal general's office within five days after the end of the month to

which they relate; and one copy thereof will be kept on file by each provost marshal.

99. Officers, in signing accounts and papers, must give their rank and regiment, or corps. Provost marshals must append their title to their names.

100. No expenditure must be charged without a proper voucher to support it.

101. Each voucher must be separately entered on the abstract of indebtedness incurred.

102. Each voucher should be complete in itself, being accompanied by all orders and explanations necessary to make it fully understood.

103. Vouchers for purchases must specify the date and place of purchase, the items and amount, and the name of the person or persons in whose favor the account is made.

104. Vouchers for other expenditures must specify when, where, to whom, and for what purpose the expenditure was made; the number and names of the persons for whom the expense was incurred—if for officers or enlisted men, the company and regiment to which they belong. When the names are numerous, a separate list of them should accompany the voucher.

105. Vouchers must, in all cases, be *accompanied by the receipt* of the party to whom payment is made, and by the certificate of an officer of the army or provost marshal, that the amount charged is accurate and just, and that it was necessary for the public service.

106. When a voucher is not supported by a certificate of an officer or provost marshal, it must be accompanied by the affidavit of the person incurring the expense, setting forth that it was actually and necessarily incurred in the public service.

107. The *receipt to a voucher* must be signed, when practicable, by a principal. When this is not practicable, the provost marshal will add, to his own certificate, a statement that the agent is duly authorized to sign the receipt.

108. When an individual makes "his mark," instead of signing his name to the receipt, it must be witnessed by a third person.

109. If medical attendance be necessary, and there be no army surgeon available, the provost marshal may engage the services of a physician, by contract, on reasonable terms, "by the visit" or by the month.

110. In vouchers for medical attendance and medicines the name of each patient, date of, and charge for each visit, and for medicines furnished must be given, and the certificate of the physician added that the rates charged are the usual rates of the place.

111. To each voucher for notices inserted in newspapers or posters a copy of the notice or poster will be appended.

112. Vouchers to accounts which are to be paid by a disbursing officer of the quartermaster's or the subsistence departments must be made out in *quadruplicate.* Three for the use of the departments, the other for the provost marshal general.

113. Vouchers to accounts which are to be paid by the provost marshal general's department will be made out in *duplicate.*

114. Expenditures must be confined to items stated in these regulations. In an unforeseen emergency, requiring a deviation from this rule, a full explanation must be appended to the voucher for the expenditure; and if this be not satisfactory, the account will be charged against the provost marshal.

115. Among expenses proper to be incurred for the provost marshal's department may be enumerated—

1. Rent of office for district provost marshals.
2. Purchase of necessary fuel for office of district provost marshals.
3. Subsistence of drafted men while at rendezvous; not to exceed thirty cents *per diem*, in case subsistence cannot be furnished by subsistence department.
4. Necessary transportation of drafted men to rendezvous, and to their homes in case of discharge, at the rate of (not to exceed) two cents per mile for railroad travel, and at the current rates for stage and steamboat fare.
5. Knives, forks, spoons, tin cups, and tin plates for drafted men.
6. Necessary medicines and medical attendance, as provided for in the regulations.
7. Actual necessary expenses incurred in arrest of spies, deserters, &c., by authorized agents of provost marshals.
8. Advertising in (not to exceed two) newspapers, in the city or district, the necessary notices, &c., concerning the draft.
9. Such other necessary expenses, not herein provided for, as may be deemed necessary to the efficient execution of the duties of provost marshal, subject to the decision of the provost marshal general.

116. Accounts, returns, and reports, except tri-monthly reports, must be accompanied by a letter of transmittal, enumerating them, and referring to no other subject.

117. All copies of papers to accompany letters or accounts should be certified by an *officer* as "true copies."

118. All accounts for jail-fees and lodging of deserters, or for the transportation of the guards or parties in charge of them, shall be rendered to the provost marshal, and shall be examined by him; if found correct and reasonable, he shall make out separate vouchers (Forms 12, 15) for each account and sign the certificate thereon.

119. One copy of the voucher will be transmitted, through the provost marshal, to the provost marshal general for payment. The other copy will be retained by the provost marshal, to be forwarded, at the end of the month, with his abstract of indebtedness to the provost marshal general.

To insure prompt payment on vouchers which are not presented, in person, by the party to whom the account is due, the receipt on the vouchers should be signed by him before the vouchers are forwarded.

120. Accounts for the five dollars reward authorized for the apprehension of a deserter, and for the reasonable expenses incurred in his delivery to the nearest

provost marshal, shall be rendered and made out, and one voucher retained and disposed of, as prescribed for the accounts in the preceding paragraph.

121. Triplicates of these vouchers will be given to the person to whom the account is due for presentation to the nearest disbursing officer of the quartermaster's department for payment, or if he choose he may have the vouchers forwarded to the provost marshal general, as already prescribed for other accounts.

122. When it becomes absolutely necessary to purchase subsistence for prisoners, deserters, or guards en route from a station to the place of destination, or whilst travelling on duty, the bills must be paid and receipts obtained for the amounts by the district provost marshal or by the special provost marshal in charge of the party, to whom the amounts will be reimbursed on presenting their accounts made out on proper vouchers.—(Form 15.)

123. The original bills (Form 16) for subsistence furnished *en route* must be kept as *sub-vouchers* to the account for reimbursement, must be made out in quadruplicate, and must specify the place and date of expenditure, the items and amounts, the number and names of the party subsisted; and if enlisted men, their company and regiment; must be *accompanied* by the receipt of the person to whom payment was made, and by the affidavit of the person incurring the expense that it was actually and necessarily incurred in the public service.

124. Vouchers to accounts for reimbursement (Form 15) will be made out and certified by the district provost marshal, and must specify the place and date of expenditure, the number and names of the prisoners, deserters, and guards, and the period for which the expense was incurred.

125. When the expenditures have been incurred for enlisted men, triplicates of the above vouchers with their corresponding sub-vouchers will be given to the person claiming reimbursement, to be presented or sent to the nearest disbursing officer of the subsistence department for payment.

The fourth voucher and sub-voucher will be retained and disposed of as provided in paragraph 119.

126. When the expense has been incurred for civilians the vouchers and sub-vouchers will be sent for payment direct to the provost marshal general.

127. The vouchers (Form 18) in quadruplicate will be made out and certified by the provost marshal, and will be disposed of as indicated for other accounts.

128. Vouchers for office-rent and for the rent of rendezvous, (Form 18;) for the purchase of office furniture, fuel, and stationery, (Form 13;) for postage, (Form 14;) and for travelling pay to drafted persons, (Form 11;) and for the payment of persons employed, (Form 17,) to be sent monthly, after being properly made out, certified, and receipted, will be forwarded for payment direct to the provost marshal general. One copy of these vouchers to be retained, except 17, and disposed of as provided in paragraph 119.

129. All accounts for per diem to special provost marshals, special guards, and to all other persons for services rendered, and not herein otherwise specially provided for, will be made out and certified by the provost marshal, and shall be disposed of as provided in paragraph 119.

130. The expenses incurred for drafted persons prior to their reporting for duty, and for deserters previous to their delivery at a provost marshal's rendezvous, including subsistence while at the rendezvous, must be paid by the provost marshal general from the appropriations at his disposal; but after leaving the rendezvous to join their regiments or any general rendezvous established by the War Department, all expenses for the subsistence and transportation of drafted persons and deserters shall be paid by the subsistence and quartermaster's departments, respectively.

131. All questions relating to the payment of expenses connected with the enrolment and draft, the arrest and return of deserters to their regiments, or such other duties as provost marshals shall be called upon to perform, shall be referred to the provost marshal general, whose decision thereon shall, so far as the War Department is concerned, be final.

---

[Extracts from General Regulations of the Army.]

## ARTICLE XLI.

### PUBLIC PROPERTY, MONEY, ACCOUNTS, AND CONTRACTS.

995. Any officer who shall directly or indirectly sell or dispose of, for a premium, any treasury note, draft, warrant, or other public security in his hands for disbursement, or sell or dispose of the proceeds or avails thereof without making returns of such premium and accounting therefor by charging it in his accounts to the credit of the United States, will forthwith be dismissed by the President.—(Act August 6, 1846.)

996. If any disbursing officer shall bet at cards or any game of hazard, his commanding officer shall suspend his functions, and require him to turn over all the public funds in his keeping, and shall immediately report the case to the proper bureau of the War Department.

997. All officers are forbid to give or take any receipt in blank for public money or property; but in all cases the voucher shall be made out in full, and the true date, place, and exact amount of money, in words, shall be written out in the receipt before it is signed.

1000. No officer disbursing or directing the disbursement of money for the military service shall be concerned, directly or indirectly, in the purchase or sale, for commercial purposes, of any article intended for, making a part of, or appertaining to the department of the public service in which he is engaged, nor shall take, receive, or apply to his own use any gain or emolument, under the guise of presents or otherwise, for negotiating or transacting any public business, other than what is or may be allowed by law.

1002. No officer or agent in the military service shall purchase from any other person in the military service, or make any contract with any such person to furnish supplies or services, or make any purchase or contract in which such person shall be admitted to any share or part, or to any benefit to arise therefrom.

1003. No person in the military service whose salary, pay, or emoluments is or are fixed by law or regulations, shall receive any additional pay, extra allowance, or compensation, in any form whatever, for the disbursement of public money, or any other service or duty whatsoever, unless the same shall be authorized by law, and explicitly set out in the appropriation.

1004. All accounts of expenditures shall set out a sufficient explanation of the object, necessity, and propriety of the expenditure.

1005. The facts on which an account depends must be stated and vouched by the certificate of an officer, or other sufficient evidence.

1006. If any account paid on the certificate of an officer to the facts is afterwards disallowed for error of fact in the certificate, it shall pass to the credit of the disbursing officer, and be charged to the officer who gave the certificate.

1007. An officer shall have credit for an expenditure of money or property made in obedience to the order of his commanding officer. If the expenditure is disallowed, it shall be charged to the officer who ordered it.

1009. When a disbursing officer is relieved, he shall certify the outstanding debts to his successor, and transmit an account of the same to the head of the bureau, and turn over his public money and property appertaining to the service from which he is relieved, to his successor, unless otherwise ordered.

1014. No officer has authority to insure public property or money.

1015. Disbursing officers are not authorized to settle with heirs, executors, or administrators, except by instructions from the proper bureau of the War Department upon accounts duly audited and certified by the proper accounting officers of the treasury.

1017. No public property shall be used, nor labor hired for the public be employed, for any private use whatsoever not authorized by the regulations of the service.

1027. If any article of public property be lost or damaged by neglect or fault of any officer or soldier, he shall pay the value of such article, or amount of damage, or cost of repairs, at such rates as a board of survey, with the approval of the commanding officer, may assess, according to the place and circumstances of the loss or damage. And he shall, moreover, be proceeded against as the Articles of War provide, if he demand a trial by court-martial, or the circumstances should require it.

1029. If any article of public property be embezzled, or by neglect lost or damaged, by any person hired in the public service, the value or damage, as ascertained, if necessary, by a board of survey, shall be charged to him, and set against any pay or money due him.

1030. Public property lost or destroyed in the military service must be accounted for by affidavit, or the certificate of a commissioned officer, or other satisfactory evidence.

1031. Affidavits or depositions may be taken before any officer in the list, as follows, when recourse cannot be had to any before named on said list, which fact shall be certified by the officer offering the evidence: 1st, a civil magistrate competent to administer oaths; 2d, a judge advocate; 3d, the recorder of a garrison or regimental court-martial; 4th, the adjutant of a regiment; 5th, a commissioned officer.

1033. No officer making returns of property shall drop from his return any public property as worn out or unserviceable until it has been condemned, after proper inspection, and ordered to be so dropped.

1053. It is the duty of every commanding officer to enforce a rigid economy in the public expenses.

## LIST OF FORMS.

No. 1. Tri-monthly report of persons arrested.
No. 2. Tri-monthly report of deserters arrested.
No. 3. Monthly abstract of indebtedness.
No. 4. Monthly report of persons and articles employed.
No. 5. Monthly report of persons arrested.
No. 6. Monthly returns of provost marshals' parties and deserters.
No. 7. Monthly return of public property.
No. 8. Abstract of articles purchased.
No. 9. Abstract of articles expended, &c.
No. 10. List of articles expended, lost, &c.
No. 11. Travelling pay to drafted persons.
No. 12. Transportation of deserters, &c.
No. 13. Purchases.
No. 14. Postage, &c.
No. 15. Reimbursements of expenses paid.
No. 16. Sub-voucher to claim for reimbursement.
No. 17. Receipt-roll of persons employed.
No. 18. General voucher.
No. 19. Abstract of lodgings.
No. 20. Contract for subsistence.
No. 21. Voucher for purchase of rations.
No. 22. Abstracts of rations issued.
No. 23. Return of lodgings.
No. 24. Return of rations.
No. 25. Exemption for son of widow, or aged or infirm parents.
No. 26. Exemption for one of two sons of aged or infirm parents.
No. 27. Exemption for only brother of dependent child or children.
No. 28. Exemption on account of two members of family being in military service.
No. 29. Exemption for father of dependent motherless children.
No. 30. Exemption for unsuitableness of age.
No. 31. Certificate of non-liability to military duty.
No. 32. Certificate of disability.
No. 33. Certificate of discharge.
No. 34. Descriptive roll of drafted men.
No. 35. Enrolment list, class I.
No. 36. Consolidated enrolment list, class I.
No. 37. Enrolment list, class II.
No. 38. Consolidated enrolment list, class II.
No. 39. Notification to persons of their having been drafted.

## Form 1.

*Tri-monthly report of persons arrested in ———, district of ———, from the ——— day of ——— to the ——— day of ———, 186–.*

[This report will be sent direct to the provost marshal general on the 10th, 20th, and last days of each month, and a copy to the acting assistant provost marshal general of each State.]

| | Remaining in custody at last report. | Number arrested during the last ten days. | Number disposed of. | Remaining in custody of provost marshal or civil authorities. | How disposed of. | | | | | Remarks. |
|---|---|---|---|---|---|---|---|---|---|---|
| | | | | | Sent to ———. | Sent to ———. | Sent to ———. | Sent to ———. | | |
| | | | | | | | | | | |

Date ———.
Station ———.

——— ———,
*Provost Marshal.*

## Form 2.

*Tri-monthly report of deserters arrested in ———, district of ———, from the ——— day of ——— to the ——— day of ———, 186–.*

[This report will be sent direct to the provost marshal general on the 10th, 20th, and last days of each month, and a copy to the acting assistant provost marshal general of the State.]

| | Remaining in custody at last report. | Number arrested during the last ten days. | Number disposed of. | Remaining in custody of provost marshal or civil authorities. | How disposed of. | | | | | Remarks. |
|---|---|---|---|---|---|---|---|---|---|---|
| | | | | | Sent to ———. | Sent to ———. | Sent to ———. | Sent to ———. | | |
| | | | | | | | | | | |

Date ———.
Station ———.

——— ———,
*Provost Marshal.*

## Form 3.

*Abstract of indebtedness incurred by ——— ———, provost marshal of the ——— district of ———, for ———, 186–.*

| Date. | No. of voucher. | To whom indebted. | On what account. | Amount. | |
|---|---|---|---|---|---|
| | | | | Dollars. | Cents. |
| | | | | | |
| | | | $ | | |

I certify that the above abstract is correct.

——— ———,
*Provost Marshal.*

[Duplicates.]
Date ———.
Station ———.

### Form 4.

*Report of persons and articles employed and hired in the ——— district of ———, during the month of ———, 186—, by ——— ———, provost marshal.*

| Running numbers. | Names of persons and articles. | Designation and occupation. | Service during the month. | | | Rate of hire or compensation. | | | Date of contract, agreement, or entry into service. | By whom owned. | Am't of rent or pay in the mo. | | Remarks. Showing by whom the buildings were occupied, and for what purpose, and how the men were employed during the month. Transfers and discharges will be noted under this head. | Time, and the amount due and remaining unpaid. | | | |
|---|---|---|---|---|---|---|---|---|---|---|---|---|---|---|---|---|---|
| | | | From | To | Days | Dolls. | Cts. | Days or month. | | | Dolls. | Cts. | | From— | To— | Dolls. | Cts. |
| | | | | | | | | | | | | | | | | | |
| Amount of rent and hire during the month.................................................. | | | | | | | | | | | | | Total amount due and remaining unpaid.... | | | | |

I certify, on honor, the above is a true report of all the persons and articles employed and hired by me during the month of ——, 186–, and that the observations under the head of "Remarks," and the statement of amounts due and remaining unpaid, are correct.

—— ——, *Provost Marshal.*

Date ——.

Station ——.

FORM 5.

*Monthly report of persons arrested in ———, district of ———, for the month of ———, 186 .*

| | Remaining in custody last report. | Number arrested during the month. | Number disposed of. | Remaining in custody of provost marshal, or civil authorities. | HOW DISPOSED OF. | | | | | Remarks. |
|---|---|---|---|---|---|---|---|---|---|---|
| | | | | | Sent to ———. | Sent to ———. | Sent to ———. | Sent to ———. | | |
| | | | | | | | | | | |

Date ———.

Station ———.

——— ———,
*Provost Marshal.*

### FORM 6.

*Return of the provost marshal's party, and of deserters under charge of —— ——, provost marshal of the —— district of ——, for the month of ——, 186 .*

| PARTY AND DESERTERS. | | | | | | | | | | | | | | | | | | | ALTERATIONS SINCE LAST RETURN. | | | | | | | | | | | | | Remarks. |
|---|---|---|---|---|---|---|---|---|---|---|---|---|---|---|---|---|---|---|---|---|---|---|---|---|---|---|---|---|---|---|---|---|
| PRESENT. | | | | | | | | | | | ABSENT. | | | | PRESENT AND ABSENT | | | | JOINED. | | | | TRANSFERRED. | | | | DISCHARGED. | | | | | |
| Belonging to the party. | | | | | | | | | Enlisted men. | | With leave. | | Without leave. | | | | | | Party. | | | | Party. | | | | Party. | | | | | |
| Provost marshal. | Captains. | Subalterns. | Sergeants. | Corporals. | Musicians. | Privates. | Deserters. | Commissioned officers. | Belonging to the party. | Deserters. | Commissioned officers. | Enlisted men. | Commissioned officers. | Enlisted men. | Commissioned officers. | Enlisted men, (party and deserters.) | Aggregate. | Aggregate last return. | By enlistment. | From other stations. | From civil authority. | From desertion. | To other stations. | To regiments. | To civil authority. | To military posts. | By expiration of service. | For disability. | By civil authority. | Died. | Deserted from the station. | NOTE 1.—The day on which an officer joins, is transferred, or relieved, will be here inserted. |
| | | | | | | | | | | | | | | | | | | | | | | | | | | | | | | | | |

*Names of enlisted men required, in explanation of "alterations since last return," &c.*

| No. | Names.—(See note 2.) | Comp'y. | Regiment. | Date of joining. | Date of transfer. | Date of discharge. | Date of death. | Date of desertion. | Where transferred. | |
|---|---|---|---|---|---|---|---|---|---|---|
| | | | | | | | | | | NOTE 2.—The names of the party and of the deserters must be kept separate. |

Date ——.
Station ——.

—— ——, *Provost Marshal.*

## Form 7.

*Return of public property received, issued, and remaining on hand in the —— district of ———, during the month of ———, 186 , by —— ———, provost marshal.*

| From whom received. | Date. | No. of voucher, &c. | STATIONERY. | | | | | | OFFICE FURNITURE, ETC. | | | | | | Remarks. | |
|---|---|---|---|---|---|---|---|---|---|---|---|---|---|---|---|---|
| | | | Letter paper, quires. | Envelopes. | Pens. | | | | Desks. | Tables. | Chairs. | | Straw, lbs. | Coal, lbs. | | |
| On hand, per last return.........<br>Received from ———. ...... ...<br>Purchased, per abstract ......... | | | | | | | | | | | | | | | | NOTE.—Vouchers for purchases are not required with this return; but all property, of whatever kind, if purchased with funds from the provost marshal general's department, will be taken up on this return. |
| Total to be accounted for........ | | | | | | | | | | | | | | | | |
| Transferred to ———............<br>Expended, per abstract.......... | | | | | | | | | | | | | | | | |
| Total issued and expended ...... | | | | | | | | | | | | | | | | |
| Remaining on hand. ............ | | | | | | | | | | | | | | | | |

I certify that the above return is correct, and that the articles specified were actually and necessarily expended in the public service.

(DUPLICATES.)

—— ———, *Provost Marshal.*

Date ———.

Station ———.

# Form 8.

*Abstract of articles purchased in the* ——, *district of* ——, *in the month of* ——, 186 , *by* —— ——, *provost marshal.*

| Date. | No. of voucher. | CLASSES. | | | FUEL. | | | | STATIONERY. | | | | | | | | | | | | OFFICE FURNITURE. | | | | | |
|---|---|---|---|---|---|---|---|---|---|---|---|---|---|---|---|---|---|---|---|---|---|---|---|---|---|---|
| | | From whom purchased. | Amount | | Wood. | | | Coal. | Letter paper. | Cap paper. | Envelope paper. | Envelopes. | Black ink. | Red ink. | Wafers. | Steel pens. | Tape. | Lead pencils. | | | Tables. | Chairs. | Desks. | Inkstands. | Rulers. | |
| | | | Dollars. | Cents. | Cords. | Feet. | Inches. | Bushels. | Qrs. | Qrs. | Qrs. | No. | Botls. | Botls. | Ozs. | No. | Pcs. | No. | | | No. | No. | No. | No | No. | |
| | | | | | | | | | | | | | | | | | | | | | | | | | | |
| Articles purchased and paid for... | | | | | | | | | | | | | | | | | | | | | | | | | | |
| | | | | | | | | | | | | | | | | | | | | | | | | | | |
| Articles purchased and not paid for. | | | | | | | | | | | | | | | | | | | | | | | | | | |
| Total purchased within the month. | | | | | | | | | | | | | | | | | | | | | | | | | | |

Note.—This abstract appertains exclusively to the *return of public property*. Must show all the articles purchased, *whether paid for or not*. Vouchers for the purchases will be sent with the *abstract of indebtedness* incurred.

I certify that the above abstract is correct.

—— ——, *Provost Marshal.*

Date ——
Station ——.

## FORM 9.

*Abstract of articles expended, lost, destroyed, &c., in the public service, in the ——— district of ———, in the month of ———, 186–.*

| Classes. | | | Fuel. | Stationery. | | | | Office furniture. | | | |
|---|---|---|---|---|---|---|---|---|---|---|---|
| Date. | No. of certificate. | By whom made. | | | | | | | | | |
| | | | | | | | | | | | |
| Total....... .............. | | | | | | | | | | | |

I certify that the above abstract is correct.

———— ————,
*Provost Marshal.*

Date ———.
Station ———.

## FORM 10.

*List of articles expended, lost, destroyed, in the public service, in the ——— district of ———, while in the possession and charge of ——— ———, provost marshal, in the month of ———, 186—.*

| Number or quantity. | Articles. | Circumstances and cause. |
|---|---|---|
| | | |

I certify that the several articles of public property above enumerated have been necessarily expended and unavoidably lost or destroyed while in the public service, as indicated by the remarks annexed to them respectively-

———— ————,
*Provost Marshal.*

NOTE.—Separate lists will be made of the articles expended, lost, &c.

Date ———.
Station ———.

## FORM 11.

*Travelling pay to drafted persons.*

## Form 12.

### *Transportation of deserters, &c.*

THE UNITED STATES To —— ——, DR.

| 186 . | | Dollars. | Cents. |
|---|---|---|---|
| | For transportation of 40 deserters (or drafted persons) en route to —— from —— to ——, being 400 miles, at $—— each.................. | | |

I certify that the above account is correct and just; the services were rendered as stated, and were necessary for the public service; the deserters (or drafted persons) are named on my return for the month of ——, 186 .

Date ——.

Station ——.

—— ——,
*Provost Marshal.*

Received, at ——, the —— of ——, 186—, of —— ——, the sum of —— dollars and —— cents, in full of the above account.

—— ——.

(QUADRUPLICATES.)

NOTE.—This voucher must be made in name of company or person furnishing the transportation, and must show ——.

---

## Form 13.

### *Purchases.*

THE UNITED STATES To —— ——, DR.

| Date. | For— | | |
|---|---|---|---|
| | 5 cords of wood.................................... | | |
| | 300 pounds of coal.................................... | | |
| | 50 bushels of coal.................................... | | |
| | 4 quires paper.................................... | | |
| | 2 lead pencils.................................... | | |

I certify that the above account is correct and just; the articles will be accounted for on my property return for the month of ——, 186—.

Date ——.

Station ——.

—— ——,
*Provost Marshal.*

Received, at Albany, N. Y., this —— day of ——, 186—, of —— ——, —— dollars and —— cents, in full of the above account.

—— ——.

(DUPLICATES.)

NOTE.—This voucher should be made in name of person or firm furnishing the articles.

## Form 14.

### *Postage, &c.*

THE UNITED STATES To —— ——, Dr.

| 186 . | | Dollars. | Cents. |
|---|---|---|---|
| | For cash paid for postage on letters and packages on public service, received and sent by him, from the —— of ——, 186 , to the —— of ——, 186 , inclusive.................................. | | |
| | For cash paid for telegrams.......................................... | | |
| | NOTE.—Copies of telegrams must accompany voucher, and amount for each telegram must be given. | | |

I certify, on honor, that the foregoing account is correct and just; that the letters, packages, and telegrams, as above, were all on public service, and that I have actually paid the amount charged.

Date ——.

Station ——.

—— ——.

Received, at ——, the —— of ——, 186 , of —— ——, —— dollars and —— cents, in full of the above account.

—— ——.

(DUPLICATES.)

NOTE.—This voucher can be made in the name of the officer.

---

## Form 15.

THE UNITED STATES To —— ——, Provost Marshal, Dr.

| 186 . | | Dollars. | Cents. |
|---|---|---|---|
| | For reimbursement of expenses paid by him for boarding deserters and guards, (*enlisted men;*) guards, (*civilians;*) prisoners, (*civilians;*) while *en route* from —— to ——, a period of —— days. Sum paid $—— .......................... ...................... | | |
| | (See sub-vouchers annexed, form 16.) | | |

I certify that the above account is correct and just; that the expenses charged were actually incurred as stated, were necessary for the public service, and were paid by me as charged.

Date ——.

Station ——.

—— ——,
*Provost Marshal.*

Received, at ——, this —— day of ——, 186 , from Lieutenant ——, regiment of ——, A. C. S. United States army, —— dollars and —— cents, in full of the above account.

—— ——.

(TRIPLICATES.)

NOTE.—As far as may be practicable, the rank, company, and regiment of each enlisted man furnished with meals must be specifically stated in the sub-voucher hereto attached. When the expense is incurred for *civilians*, the vouchers and sub-vouchers therefor must be forwarded for payment to the provost marshal general.

## Form 16.

*(Sub-voucher to voucher 15.)*

Received, at —— this —— day of —— 186 , from ——, provost marshal, the sum of —— dollars and —— cents, for furnishing —— enlisted men, —— meals, at —— cents per meal,

| Names of enlisted men boarded. | Rank. | Company. | Regiment. | Remarks. |
|---|---|---|---|---|
| | | | | The names of *enlisted men* and *civilians* to be entered separately. |

To be supported by the affidavit of the person incurring the expense, that it was actually and necessarily incurred.

(Quadruplicates.)

---

## Form 17.

We, the subscribers, do hereby acknowledge to have received of —— the sums opposite our names, respectively, being in full of our pay for the period herein expressed, having signed duplicates hereof.

| Date. | Number. | Names. | Occupation. | Period of service. | | | | Rate of pay. | | | Amount of pay. | | Am't of stop'ges. | | Amount received | | Signer's names. | Witnesses. | Remarks. |
|---|---|---|---|---|---|---|---|---|---|---|---|---|---|---|---|---|---|---|---|
| | | | | From— | To— | Months. | Days. | Dollars. | Cents. | Per month, or day. | Dollars. | Cents. | Dollars. | Cents. | Dollars. | Cents. | | | |
| | | | | | | | | | | | — | — | — | — | — | — | | | |

I certify that the above receipt-roll is correct and just.

Date ——.

Station ——.

—— ——, *Provost Marshal*, —— *district of* ——.

## Form 18.

The United States To —— ——, Dr.

| 186 . | | Dollars. | Cents. |
|---|---|---|---|
| | | | |
| | $ | | |

I certify, on honor, that the above account is correct and just; that the services were rendered as stated, and were necessary for the public service.

Date ——.

Station ——.

—— ——,
*Provost Marshal.*

Received, at ——, this —— day of ——, 186—, from —— ——, —— ——, —— dollars and —— cents, in full of the above account.

—— ——.

(Signed in duplicate or quadruplicate.)

Notes.—"All accounts of expenditures shall set out a sufficient explanation of the object, necessity, and propriety of the expenditure."

The dates between which employed, rate of pay per day or month, and if the person employed be in the military service, his rank, company, and regiment, should all be specifically stated.

"The facts on which an account depends must *be stated and vouched* by the certificate of an officer or other *sufficient* evidence."

When a receipt is signed by a mark, it must be witnessed, and by a third person.

This form will be used in cases where no other is prescribed.

## Form 19.

*Abstract of lodgings furnished to provost marshal's party, in the —— district of ——, under charge of —— ——, provost marshal, from —— to ——, by —— ——, special contractor.*

| Date. | No. of return. | No. of men. | Commencing. | Ending. | No. of days drawn for. | Total. | Remarks. |
|---|---|---|---|---|---|---|---|
| | | | | | | | |
| Total number.............................................. | | | | | | | |

I certify that I have carefully compared the above abstract with the original returns now in my possession, and find the abstract correct.

—— ——,
*Provost Marshal.*

Note.—An abstract of this form must accompany each voucher for payment for lodgings.

## Form 20.

Articles of Agreement, made and entered into this —— day of ——, anno Domini one thousand eight hundred and sixty——, between —— ——, provost marshal, district of ——, of the one part, and —— ——, of the county of —— and State of ——, of the other part.

*This agreement witnesseth*, That the said —— ——, for and on behalf of the United States of America, and the said —— ——, heirs, executors and administrators, have covenanted and agreed, and by these presents do mutually covenant and agree, to and with each other, as follows, viz:

*First.* That the said —— ——, heirs, executors and administrators, shall supply, or cause to be supplied and issued, at ——, all the rations, to consist of the articles hereinafter specified, that shall be required at the provost marshal's rendezvous at the place aforesaid, commencing on the —— day of ——, one thousand eight hundred and sixty——, and ending on the —— of ——, eighteen hundred and ——, or such earlie day as the provost marshal general may direct, at the price of —— cents —— mills for each complete ration.

*Second.* That the ration to be furnished by virtue of this contract shall consist of the following articles, viz: One and a quarter pound of fresh beef, or three-quarters of a pound of salted pork, eighteen ounces of bread or flour, and at the rate of eight quarts of beans or ten pounds of rice, ten pounds of coffee, fifteen pounds of sugar, four quarts of vinegar, and one and a half pounds of tallow, or one pound of sperm candles, four pounds of soap, and two quarts of salt, to every hundred rations, or the contractor shall furnish the men with good and whole-some board and lodging, at the option of the provost marshal; and the party shall have the privilege of hanging out a flag from the place of rendezvous.

*Third.* That fresh beef shall be issued at least thrice in each week, if required by the provost marshal·

*Fourth.* It is clearly understood that the provisions stipulated to be furnished and delivered under this contract shall be of the first quality.

*Fifth.* Should any difficulty arise respecting the quality of the provisions stipulated to be delivered under this contract, then the provost marshal is to appoint a disinterested person to meet one of the same description to be appointed by the contractor. These two thus appointed will have power to decide on the quality of the provisions; but should they disagree, then a third person is to be chosen by these two already appointed, the whole to act under oath, and the opinion of the majority to be final in the case.

*Sixth.* No member of Congress shall be admitted to any share herein, or any benefit to arise therefrom.

In witness whereof, the undersigned have hereunto placed their hands and seals the day and date above written.

Witness:

—— ——. [L. S.]
—— ——. [L. S.]

(Quintuplicates.)

---

## EXTRACT.

o o o o o o o o o

Sec. 13. *And be it further enacted*, That the army ration shall be increased as follows, viz: Twenty-two ounces of bread or flour, or one pound of hard bread, instead of the present issue; fresh beef shall be issued as often as the commanding officer of any detachment or regiment shall require it, when practicable, in place of salt meat; beans and rice or hominy shall be issued in the same ration in the proportions now provided by the regulation, and one pound of potatoes per man shall be issued at least three times a week, if practicable; and when these articles cannot be issued in these proportions, an equivalent in value shall be issued in some other proper food, and a ration of tea may be substituted for a ration of coffee upon the requisition of the proper officer: *Provided*, That after the present insurrection shall cease, the ration shall be as provided by law and regulations on the first day of July, eighteen hundred and sixty-one.

o o o o o o o o o

Approved August 3, 1861.

## Form 21.

The United States To —— ——, Special Contractor, Dr.

| 186 . | | | | |
|---|---|---|---|---|
| | For rations issued to provost marshal's party, under the charge of —— ——, in district of ——, from —— to ——, as per accompanying abstract: | | | |
| | —— complete rations, at —— cents................ | | | |
| | —— lbs. extra soap, at —— cents. ......... ......... | | | |
| | —— lbs. extra candles, at —— cents.... ............ | | | |
| | Due contractor.................................. ..$ | | | |

Received from —— ——, at ——, this —— day of ——, 186 , —— dollars and cents, in full of the above account.

—— ——,
*Special Contractor.*

(Duplicates.)

## Form 22.

*Abstract of rations issued to provost marshal's party, under charge of —— ——, provost marshal, from —— to ——, by —— ——, special contractor.*

| Date. | No. of return. | No. of men. | Commencing. | Ending. | No. of days drawn for. | No. of complete rations. | Remarks. |
|---|---|---|---|---|---|---|---|
| | | | | | | | |
| Total number of complete rations..................... | | | | | | | |

I certify that I have carefully compared the above abstract with the original returns now in my possession, and they amount to —— complete rations.

Date ——.

Station ——.

—— ——,
*Provost Marshal.*

(Duplicates.)

FORM 23.

*Return of lodgings furnished to provost marshal's party (or ——— ———) in the —— district of ———, under charge of ——— ———, provost marshal, from ——— to ———, by ——— ———, special contractor.*

| Date. | No. of return. | No. of men. | Commencing. | Ending. | No. of days drawn for. | Total. | Remarks. |
|---|---|---|---|---|---|---|---|
| | | | | | | | |

I certify that the above return is correct.

——— ———,
*Provost Marshal.*

FORM 24.

*Provision return for —— days, commencing on the —— of ——— and ending on the —— of ———.*

| Date. | No. of return. | No. of men. | Commencing. | Ending. | No. of days drawn for. | No. of complete rations. | Remarks. |
|---|---|---|---|---|---|---|---|
| | | | | | | | |

I certify that the above return is correct.

Date ——.

Station ——.

——— ———,
*Provost Marshal.*

### Form 25.

*Certificate of exemption for the son of a widow, or of aged and infirm parent or parents.*

I, the subscriber, ————, resident of ————, ———— county, State of ————, hereby certify that I, ————, being liable to military duty under the act of Congress "for enrolling and calling out the national forces," &c., approved March 3, 1863, am the only son of ————, a widow, (or of ————, an aged parent,) dependent on my labor for support.

———— ————.

We, the subscribers, do hereby certify that the above-named ———— is the only son of a widow, (or of aged and infirm parents,) dependent on his labor for support.

———— ————.

———— ————.

Personally appeared before me, ————, the above named ————, and ————, and severally made oath that the above certificate is correct and true, to the best of their knowledge and belief.

———— ————,
*Justice of the Peace.*

Dated this —— day of ————, 186—.

Note 1.—The first of the above certificates must be signed by the person claiming exemption, and the second by two respectable citizens (heads of families) residents of the town, county, or district, in which the person resides, and sworn to before a magistrate.

Note 2.—This certificate is to be used only in cases where the *labor* of the person claiming exemption is actually necessary for the support of the persons dependent on him. The exemption does not apply in cases where there is sufficient property to yield support, and the necessary business for collecting the income can be transacted by agents, trustees, or the like.

---

### Form 26.

*Certificate of a parent that he or she desires one of his or her sons exempted.*

I, the subscriber, the father (or mother) of ———— and ————, residents of ————, ———— county, State of ————, hereby certify that I am aged and infirm, and that I am dependent for support on the labor of my two sons, above named; and that I elect that my ———— son ————, shall be exempt from the operations of the act of Congress "for enrolling and calling out the national forces," &c., approved March 3, 1863.

———— ————.

We, the subscribers, do hereby certify that the above named ————, is aged and infirm, and dependent on the labor of ———— sons for support.

———— ————.

———— ————.

Personally appeared before me, the above named ————, ———— and ————, and severally made oath that the above certificates are correct and true, to the best of their knowledge and belief.

———— ————,
*Justice of the Peace.*

Dated at ————, this ———— day of ————, 186—.

Note 1.—The first certificate must be signed by the parent making the election, and the second by two respectable citizens (heads of families) residents of the town, county, or district in which the persons reside, and sworn to before a magistrate. In case the father is deceased the certificate is to be signed by the mother, and the fact of the father's death is to be stated by the persons certifying.

Note 2.—This certificate is to be used only in cases where the *labor* of the person claiming exemption is actually necessary for the support of the persons dependent on him. The exemption does not apply in cases where there is sufficient property to yield support, and the necessary business for collecting the income can be transacted by agents, trustees, or the like.

## Form 27.

*Certificate that the person liable to draft is the only brother of a child or children dependent on his labor for support.*

I, the subscriber, ———————, being liable to draft into the service of the United States, hereby make affidavit that I am the only brother of ———————, under 12 years of age, having neither father nor mother, and dependent on my labor for support.

——————— —————.

We, the subscribers, ———————————, and ——————————, residents of ———————, ——————— county, State of ———————, hereby certify that ——————————, who is liable to draft, is the only brother of ———————————, under 12 years of age, having neither father nor mother, and dependent on his labor for support.

——————— —————.

——————— —————.

Personally appeared before me, the above named ——————— and ———————, and severally made oath that the above certificate is correct and true, to the best of their knowledge and belief.

——————— —————,

*Justice of the Peace.*

Dated at ———, this ——— day of ———, 186—.

Note 1.—This certificate is to be used only in cases where the *labor* of the person claiming exemption is actually necessary for the support of the persons dependent on him. The exemption does not apply in cases where there is sufficient property to yield support, and the necessary business can be transacted for collecting the income by agents, trustees, or the like.

Note 2.—The first certificate must be signed by the person claiming exemption, and the second by two respectable persons (heads of families) resident in the same town, county, or district with the person for whom exemption is claimed.

---

## Form 28.

*Certificate that two members of the family of the person liable to draft are already in the military service of the United States.*

We, the subscribers, ——————————— and ——————————, residents of ———————, ——————— county, State of ———————, hereby certify that two members of the family and household of ———————, county and State abovementioned, are in the military service of the United States, as non-commissioned officers, musicians, or privates.

——————— —————.

——————— —————.

Personally appeared before me, the above named ——————— and ———————, and severally made oath that the above certificate is correct and true, to the best of their knowledge and belief.

——————— —————,

*Justice of the Peace.*

Dated at ———————, this ——— day of ———————, 186—.

Note 1.—This is only intended to apply where the members of the family claiming exemption reside in the same family. If any of the members reside elsewhere, and have gone into the military service of the United States, no exemption on that account can be claimed.

Note 2.—This certificate must be signed by one of the parents, if there be any; if not, by two respectable persons (heads of families) resident in the same town, county, or district with the person for whom exemption is claimed.

## Form 29.

*Certificate that the person liable to draft is the father of motherless children, under 12 years of age, dependent on his labor for support.*

I, ————————, the subscriber, being liable to draft into the service of the United States, hereby make affidavit that I am the father of ——— motherless child—, under 12 years of age, and dependent on my labor for support.

———————— ————.

We, the subscribers, ————— and —————, residents of —————, ————— county, State of —————, hereby certify that ————— is father of ——— motherless children under 12 years of age, and dependent on his labor for support.

———————— ————.

———————— ————.

Personally appeared before me, the above named ————— and —————, and severally made oath that the above certificate is correct and true to the best of their knowledge and belief.

———————— ————,

*Justice of the Peace.*

Dated this ——— day of —————, 186—.

Note.—The first certificate must be signed by the person claiming exemption, and the second by two respectable persons (heads of families) resident in the same town, county, or district with the person for whom exemption is claimed.

---

## Form 30.

*Certificate for exemption on account of unsuitableness of age.*

I, —————, of —————, ————— county, State of —————, having been enrolled under the provisions of an act of Congress "for enrolling and calling out the national forces," &c., approved March 3, 1863, as liable to perform military duty in the service of the United States, hereby certify that I am not legally subject to such liability, and for the following reason:

That I am ————— years of age.

———————— ————.

We, the subscribers, ————— and —————, of the town, county, and State abovementioned, hereby certify that the above statement of —————'s age is correct and true to the best of our knowledge and belief.

———————— ————.

———————— ————.

Personally appeared before me, the above named —————, —————, and —————, and severally made oath that the above certificates are correct and true, to the best of their knowledge and belief.

———————— ————,

*Justice of the Peace.*

Dated at —————, this ——— day of —————, 186—.

Note 1.—The certificate in regard to age is, in all cases where practicable, to be signed by the parents of the person claiming exemption, and the requirements specified in the regulations are to be adhered to. The blank space in the certificate to indicate the age of the person is to be filled as follows:

That I am "under twenty" years of age.
That I am "over thirty-five" years of age, "and married."
That I am "over forty-five" years of age, according to the facts in the case.

Note 2.—In case the certificate is not signed by the parents, the fact of age must be certified to by two respectable persons (heads of families) resident in the same town, county, or district with the person for whom exemption is claimed, and the requirements of paragraph 61, Regulations, &c., must be complied with.

## Form 31.

*Certificate of non-liability to be given by the board of enrolment.*

We, the subscribers, composing the board of enrolment of the ———— district, of the State of ————, provided for in section 8, act of Congress "for enrolling and calling out the national forces," approved March 3, 1863, hereby certify that ————, of ————, ———— county, State of ————, having given satisfactory evidence that he is not properly subject to do military duty, as required by said act, by reason of ————, is exempt from all liability to military duty for the term of ————.

———— ————,
*Provost Marshal and President of Board of Enrolment.*

———— ————,
*Member of Board of Enrolment.*

———— ————,
*Surgeon of Board of Enrolment.*

Dat at ————, this ———— day of ————, 186—.

Note.—This certificate is to be given in all cases where it is applicable, according to the 2d, 3d, 13th, and 17th sections of the act of Congress referred to above.

---

## Form 32.

*Certificate of exemption for a drafted person on account of disability.*

This is to certify that ————, of ————, ———— county, State of ————, having been drafted, and claiming exemption on account of disability, has been carefully examined, and is found to be unfit for military duty by reason of ————, and, in consequence thereof, he is exempt from service under the present draft.

———— ————,
*Provost Marshal and President of Board of Enrolment.*

———— ————,
*Member of Board of Enrolment.*

———— ————,
*Surgeon of Board of Enrolment.*

Dated at ————, this ———— day of ————, 186—.

## Form 33.

*Certificate of discharge on account of the required number having been obtained.*

This is to certify that ————————, of ————————, ———— county, State of ————————, having been drafted, on the ————————, and having reported at the required place of rendezvous, is hereby "discharged" from service under that draft, on account of the required number of able-bodied men having been obtained from the names preceding his on the list of drafted men.

———— ————,
*Provost Marshal and President of Board of Enrolment.*

———— ————,
*Member of Board of Enrolment.*

———— ————,
*Surgeon of Board of Enrolment.*

Dated at ———, this ——— day of ————, 186—.

## Form 34.

*Descriptive list of drafted men called into the service of the United States.*

| No. | Names. | DESCRIPTION. | | | | | | WHERE BORN. | | Occupation. | ENROLLED. | | DRAFTED. | | Remarks. |
|---|---|---|---|---|---|---|---|---|---|---|---|---|---|---|---|
| | | Age. | Eyes. | Hair. | Complexion. | Feet. | Inches. | State or kingdom. | Town or country. | | When. | Where. | When. | Where. | |
| | | | | | | | | | | | | | | | |

We certify that the above is a correct transcript of the roll of names of persons drafted into the service of the United States from the ——— district, State of ————, on the ————, ————, in the order in which they were drawn.

———— ————,
*Provost Marshal, President of the Board of Enrolment.*

———— ————,
*Member of Board of Enrolment.*

———— ————,
*Surgeon of Board of Enrolment*

Dated at ———, this ——— day of ————, 186—.

FORM 35.

[Class I comprises all persons subject to do military duty between the ages of twenty and thirty-five years and all unmarried persons subject to do military duty above the age of thirty-five years and under the age of forty-five. Class II comprises all other persons subject to do military duty.]

---

*Enrolment list of all persons of class I, subject to do military duty in the —— sub-district of the ——— congressional district, consisting of the counties of ——— and ———, in the State of ———, enumerated by me on the —— day of ———, 186—.*

*Post office* ———. —— ———, *Enrolling Officer.*

| Residence. | Name. | DESCRIPTION. | | | | Place of birth. (Naming the State, Territory, or country.) | Former military service. | Remarks. |
|---|---|---|---|---|---|---|---|---|
| | | Age 1st July, 1863. | White or colored. | Profession, occupation, or trade. | Married or unmarried. | | | |
| | | | | | | | | |

To Captain —— ——, *Station:* ——. —— ——, *Enrolling Officer.*
*Date:* ——.
*Provost Marshal of the* —— *Cong. Dist. of* ——.

---

RECAPITULATION.

| Sub-districts. | Towns or wards. | Number of whites. | Number of colored. | Total number enrolled. |
|---|---|---|---|---|
| 1st sub-district...... | Town of ——............................ | | | |
| | Town of ——............................ | | | |
| | Town of ——............................ | | | |
| | Town of ——............................ | | | |
| 2d sub-district...... | Town of ——............................ | | | |
| | Town of ——............................ | | | |
| | Town of ——............................ | | | |
| | Town of ——............................ | | | |

## Form 36.

[Class I comprises all persons subject to do military duty between the ages of twenty and thirty-five years, and all unmarried persons subject to do military duty above the age of thirty-five years and under the age of forty-five. Class II comprises all other persons subject to do military duty.]

*Enrolment list of all persons of class II, subject to do military duty in the —— sub-district of the —— congressional district, consisting of the counties of —— and ——, in the State of ——, enumerated by me on the —— day of ——, 186—.*

*Post office* ——. —— ——, *Enrolling Officer.*

| Residence. | Name. | DESCRIPTION. | | | Place of birth. (Naming the State, Territory, or country.) | Former military service. | Remarks. |
|---|---|---|---|---|---|---|---|
| | | Age 1st July, 1863. | White or colored. | Profession, occupation, or trade. | | | |
| | | | | | | | |

To Captain —— ——, *Station:* ——. —— ——, *Enrolling Officer.*
*Date:* ——.
*Provost Marshal of the* —— *Cong. Dist. of* ——.

## RECAPITULATION.

| Sub-districts. | Towns or wards. | Number of whites. | Number of colored. | Total number enrolled. |
|---|---|---|---|---|
| 1st sub-district...... | Town of ——............................ | | | |
| | Town of ——............................ | | | |
| | Town of ——............................ | | | |
| | Town of ——............................ | | | |
| 2d sub-district ...... | Town of ——............................ | | | |
| | Town of ——............................ | | | |
| | Town of ——............................ | | | |
| | Town of ——............................ | | | |

## Form 37.

[Class I comprises all persons subject to do military duty between the ages of twenty and thirty-five years, and all unmarried persons subject to do military duty above the age of thirty five years and under the age of forty-five. Class II comprises all other persons subject to do military duty.]

*Consolidated list of all persons of class I, subject to do military duty in the —— congressional district, consisting of the counties of ——— and ———, State of ———, enumerated during the month of ——, 186—, under the direction of———, provost marshal.*

| Residence. | Name. | DESCRIPTION. | | | | Place of birth. (Naming the State, Territory, or country.) | Former military service. | Remarks. |
|---|---|---|---|---|---|---|---|---|
| | | Age 1st July, 1863. | White or colored. | Profession, occupation, or trade. | Married or unmarried. | | | |
| | | | | | | | | |

——— ———, *Provost Marshal.*

To Colonel James B. Fry, *Station: Headquarters —— Cong. Dist. of ——.*
*Provost Marshal General U. States,* *Date: ——.*
*Washington, D. C.*

### RECAPITULATION.

| Sub-districts. | Towns or wards. | Number of whites. | Number of colored. | Total number enrolled. |
|---|---|---|---|---|
| 1st sub-district ...... | Town of ——.............................. | | | |
| | Town of ——.............................. | | | |
| | Town of ——.............................. | | | |
| | Town of ——.............................. | | | |
| 2d sub-district ...... | Town of ——.............................. | | | |
| | Town of ——.............................. | | | |
| | Town of ——.............................. | | | |
| | Town of ——.............................. | | | |

Note.—The names on this consolidated list must be *alphabetically* arranged.

FORM 38.

[Class I comprises all persons subject to do military duty between the ages of twenty and thirty-five years, and all unmarried persons subject to do military duty above the age of thirty-five years and under the age of forty-five. Class II comprises all other persons subject to do military duty.]

*Consolidated list of all persons of class II, subject to do military duty in the —— congressional district, consisting of the counties of —— and ——State of ——, enumerated during the month of —— 186—, under direction of ——, provost marshal.*

| Residence. | Name. | DESCRIPTION. | | | Place of birth. (Naming the State, Territory, or country.) | Former military service. | Remarks. |
|---|---|---|---|---|---|---|---|
| | | Age 1st July, 1863. | White or colored. | Profession, occupation, or trade. | | | |
| | | | | | | | |

—— ——, *Provost Marshal.*

To Colonel JAMES B. FRY, *Provost Marshal General U. States, Washington, D. C.*

*Station:* ——. *Headquarters* —— *Cong. Dist. of* ——.
*Date:* ——.

RECAPITULATION.

| Sub-districts. | Towns or wards. | Number of whites. | Number of colored. | Total number enrolled. |
|---|---|---|---|---|
| 1st sub-district...... | Town of ——.................................... | | | |
| | Town of ——.................................... | | | |
| | Town of ——.................................... | | | |
| | Town of ——.................................... | | | |
| 2d sub-district ...... | Town of ——.................................... | | | |
| | Town of ——.................................... | | | |
| | Town of ——.................................... | | | |
| | Town of ——.................................... | | | |

NOTE.—The names on this consolidated list must be *alphabetically* arranged.

## Form 39.

Provost Marshal's Office,
——— *District, State of* ———.
——— ———, 186–.

To ——— ———,
——— ———:

Sir: You are hereby notified that you were, on the —— day of ———, 186–, legally drafted into the service of the United States for the period of ———, in accordance with the provisions of the act of Congress "for enrolling and calling out the national forces, and for other purposes," approved March 3, 1863 You will accordingly report, on the ———, at the place of rendezvous, in ———, or be deemed a deserter, and be subject to the penalty prescribed therefor by the Rules and Articles of War.

I am, sir, very respectfully, your obedient servant,

——— ———, *Provost Marshal,*
——— *District, State of* ———

# AN ACT

FOR

# ENROLLING AND CALLING OUT THE NATIONAL FORCES,

AND

# FOR OTHER PURPOSES.

---

Whereas there now exist in the United States an insurrection and rebellion against the authority thereof, and it is, under the Constitution of the United States, the duty of the government to suppress insurrection and rebellion, to guarantee to each State a republican form of government, and to preserve the public tranquillity; and whereas, for these high purposes, a military force is indispensable, to raise and support which all persons ought willingly to contribute; and whereas no service can be more praiseworthy and honorable than that which is rendered for the maintenance of the Constitution and Union, and the consequent preservation of free government: Therefore—

*Be it enacted by the Senate and House of Representatives of the United States of America in Congress assembled*, That all able-bodied male citizens of the United States, and persons of foreign birth who shall have declared on oath their intention to become citizens under and in pursuance of the laws thereof, between the ages of twenty and forty-five years, except as hereinafter excepted, are hereby declared to constitute the national forces, and shall be liable to perform military duty in the service of the United States when called out by the President for that purpose.

SEC. 2. *And be it further enacted*, That the following persons be, and they are hereby, excepted and exempt from the provisions of this act, and shall not be liable to military duty under the same, to wit: Such as are rejected as physically or mentally unfit for the service; also, first, the Vice-President of the United States, the judges of the various courts of the United States, the heads of the various executive departments of the government, and the governors of the several States. Second, the only son liable to military duty of a widow dependent upon his labor for support. Third, the only son of aged or infirm parent or parents dependent upon his labor for support. Fourth, where there are two or more sons of aged or infirm parents subject to draft, the father, or if he be dead, the mother, may elect which son shall be exempt. Fifth, the only brother of children not twelve years old, having neither father nor mother, dependent upon his labor for support. Sixth, the father of motherless children under twelve years of age, dependent upon his labor for support. Seventh, where there are a father and sons in the same family and household, and two of them are in the military service of the United States as non-commissioned officers, musicians, or privates, the residue of such family and household, not exceeding two, shall be exempt. And no persons but such as are herein excepted shall be exempt: *Provided, however,* That no person who has been convicted of any felony shall be enrolled or permitted to serve in said forces.

SEC. 3. *And be it further enacted,* That the national forces of the United States not now in the military service, enrolled under this act, shall be divided into two classes: the first of which shall comprise all persons subject to do military duty between the ages of twenty and thirty-five years, and all unmarried persons subject to do military duty above the age of thirty-five and under the age of forty-five; the second class shall comprise all other persons subject to do military duty; and they shall not, in any district, be called into the service of the United States until those of the first class shall have been called.

SEC. 4. *And be it further enacted,* That for greater convenience in enrolling, calling out, and organizing the national forces, and for the arrest of deserters and spies of the enemy, the United States shall be divided into districts, of which the District of Columbia shall constitute one, each Territory of the United States shall constitute one or more, as the President shall direct, and each congressional district of the respective States, as fixed by a law of the State next preceding the enrolment, shall constitute one: *Provided,* That in States which have not by their laws been divided into two or more congressional districts, the President of the United States shall divide the same into so many enrolment districts as he may deem fit and convenient.

SEC. 5. *And be it further enacted,* That for each of said districts there shall be appointed by the President a provost marshal, with the rank, pay, and emoluments of a captain of cavalry, or an officer of said rank shall be detailed by the President, who shall be under the direction and subject to the orders of a provost marshal general, appointed or detailed by the President of the United States, whose office shall be at the seat of government, forming a separate bureau of the War Department, and whose rank, pay, and emoluments shall be those of a colonel of cavalry.

SEC. 6. *And be it further enacted,* That it shall be the duty of the provost marshal general, with the approval of the Secretary of War, to make rules and regulations for the government of his subordinates; to furnish them with the names and residences of all deserters from the army, or any of the land forces in the service of the United States, including the militia, when reported to him by the commanding officers; to communicate to them all orders of the President in reference to calling out the national forces; to furnish proper blanks and instructions for enrolling and drafting; to file and preserve copies of all enrolment lists; to require stated reports of all proceedings on the part of his subordinates; to audit all accounts connected with the service under his direction; and to perform such other duties as the President may prescribe in carrying out the provisions of this act.

SEC. 7. *And be it further enacted,* That it shall be the duty of the provost marshals to arrest all deserters, whether regulars, volunteers, militiamen, or persons called into the service under this or any other act of Congress, wherever they may be found, and to send them to the nearest military commander or military post; to detect, seize, and confine spies of the enemy, who shall, without unreasonable delay, be delivered to the custody of the general commanding the department in which they may be arrested, to be tried as soon as the exigencies of the service permit; to obey all lawful orders and regulations of the provost marshal general, and such as may be prescribed by law, concerning the enrolment and calling into service of the national forces.

SEC. 8. *And be it further enacted,* That in each of said districts there shall be a board of enrolment, to be composed of the provost marshal, as president, and two other persons, to be appointed by the President of the United States, one of whom shall be a licensed and practicing physician and surgeon.

Sec. 9. *And be it further enacted.* That it shall be the duty of the said board to divide the district into sub-districts of convenient size, if they shall deem it necessary, not exceeding two, without the direction of the Secretary of War, and to appoint, on or before the tenth day of March next, and in each alternate year thereafter, an enrolling officer for each sub-district, and to furnish him with proper blanks and instructions; and he shall immediately proceed to enrol all persons subject to military duty, noting their respective places of residence, ages on the first day of July following, and their occupation, and shall, on or before the first day of April, report the same to the board of enrolment, to be consolidated into one list, a copy of which shall be transmitted to the provost marshal general on or before the first day of May succeeding the enrolment: *Provided, nevertheless,* That if, from any cause, the duties prescribed by this section cannot be performed within the time specified, then the same shall be performed as soon thereafter as practicable.

Sec. 10. *And be it further enacted,* That the enrolment of each class shall be made separately, and shall only embrace those whose ages shall be on the first day of July thereafter between twenty and forty-five years.

Sec. 11. *And be it further enacted,* That all persons thus enrolled shall be subject, for two years after the first day of July succeeding the enrolment, to be called into the military service of the United States, and to continue in service during the present rebellion, not, however, exceeding the term of three years; and when called into service shall be placed on the same footing, in all respects, as volunteers for three years, or during the war, including advance pay and bounty as now provided by law.

Sec. 12. *And be it further enacted,* That whenever it may be necessary to call out the national forces for military service, the President is hereby authorized to assign to each district the number of men to be furnished by said district; and thereupon the enrolling board shall, under the direction of the President, make a draft of the required number, and fifty per cent. in addition, and shall make an exact and complete roll of the names of the persons so drawn, and of the order in which they were drawn, so that the first drawn may stand first upon the said roll, and the second may stand second, and so on. And the person so drawn shall be notified of the same within ten days thereafter, by a written or printed notice, to be served personally or by leaving a copy at the last place of residence, requiring them to appear at a designated rendezvous to report for duty. In assigning to the districts the number of men to be furnished therefrom, the President shall take into consideration the number of volunteers and militia furnished by and from the several States in which said districts are situated, and the period of their service since the commencement of the present rebellion, and shall so make said assignment as to equalize the numbers among the districts of the several States, considering and allowing for the numbers already furnished as aforesaid and the time of their service.

Sec. 13. *And be it further enacted,* That any person drafted and notified to appear as aforesaid may, on or before the day fixed for his appearance, furnish an acceptable substitute to take his place in the draft; or he may pay to such person as the Secretary of War may authorize to receive it, such sum, not exceeding three hundred dollars, as the Secretary may determine, for the procuration of such substitute, which sum shall be fixed at a uniform rate by a general order made at the time of ordering a draft for any State or Territory; and thereupon such person so furnishing the substitute, or paying the money, shall be discharged from further liability under that draft. And any person failing to report after due service of notice as herein prescribed, without furnishing a substitute, or paying the required sum therefor, shall be deemed a deserter, and shall be arrested by the provost marshal, and sent to the nearest military post for trial by court-martial, unless, upon proper showing that he is not liable to do military duty, the board of enrolment shall relieve him from the draft.

SEC. 14. *And be it further enacted*, That all drafted persons shall, on arriving at the rendezvous, be carefully inspected by the surgeon of the board, who shall truly report to the board the physical condition of each one; and all persons drafted and claiming exemption from military duty on account of disability, or any other cause, shall present their claims to be exempted to the board, whose decision shall be final.

SEC. 15. *And be it further enacted*, That any surgeon charged with the duty of such inspection who shall receive from any person whomsoever any money or other valuable thing, or agree, directly or indirectly, to receive the same to his own or another's use for making an imperfect inspection or a false or incorrect report, or who shall wilfully neglect to make a faithful inspection and true report, shall be tried by a court-martial, and, on conviction thereof, be punished by fine not exceeding five hundred dollars nor less than two hundred, and be imprisoned at the discretion of the court, and be cashiered and dismissed from the service.

SEC. 16. *And be it further enacted*, That as soon as the required number of able-bodied men liable to do military duty shall be obtained from the list of those drafted, the remainder shall be discharged. And all drafted persons reporting at the place of rendezvous shall be allowed travelling pay from their places of residence; and all persons discharged at the place of rendezvous shall be allowed travelling pay to their places of residence; and all expenses connected with the enrolment and draft, including subsistence while at the rendezvous, shall be paid from the appropriation for enrolling and drafting, under such regulations as the President of the United States shall prescribe; and all expenses connected with the arrest and return of deserters to their regiments, or such other duties as the provost marshal shall be called upon to perform, shall be paid from the appropriation for arresting deserters, under such *such* regulations as the President of the United States shall prescribe: *Provided*, The provost marshals shall in no case receive commutation for transportation or for fuel and quarters, but only for forage, when not furnished by the government, together with actual expenses of postage, stationery, and clerk hire authorized by the provost marshal general.

SEC. 17. *And be it further enacted*, That any person enrolled and drafted according to the provisions of this act, who shall furnish an acceptable substitute, shall thereupon receive from the board of enrolment a certificate of dis charge from such draft, which shall exempt him from military duty during the time for which he was drafted; and such substitute shall be entitled to the same pay and allowances provided by law as if he had been originally drafted into the service of the United States.

SEC. 18. *And be it further enacted*, That such of the volunteers and militia now in the service of the United States as may re-enlist to serve one year, unless sooner discharged, after the expiration of their present term of service, shall be entitled to a bounty of fifty dollars, one-half of which to be paid upon such re-enlistment, and the balance at the expiration of the term of re-enlistment. And such as may re-enlist to serve for two years, unless sooner discharged, after the expiration of their present term of enlistment, shall receive, upon such re-enlistment, twenty-five dollars of the one hundred dollars bounty for enlistment provided by the fifth section of the act approved twenty-second of July, eighteen hundred and sixty-one, entitled "An act to authorize the employment of volunteers to aid in enforcing the laws and protecting public property."

SEC. 19. *And be it further enacted*, That whenever a regiment of volunteers of the same arm, from the same State, is reduced to one-half the maximum number prescribed by law, the President may direct the consolidation of the companies of such regiment: *Provided*, That no company so formed shall exceed the maximum number prescribed by law. When such consolidation is made, the regimental officers shall be reduced in proportion to the reduction in the number of companies.

SEC. 20. *And be it further enacted,* That whenever a regiment is reduced below the minimum number allowed by law, no officers shall be appointed in such regiment beyond those necessary for the command of such reduced number.

SEC. 21. *And be it further enacted,* That so much of the fifth section of the act approved seventeenth July, eighteen hundred and sixty-two, entitled "An act to amend an act calling forth the militia to execute the laws of the Union," and so forth, as requires the approval of the President to carry into execution the sentence of a court-martial, be, and the same is hereby, repealed, as far as relates to carrying into execution the sentence of any court-martial against any person convicted as a spy or deserter, or of mutiny or murder; and hereafter sentences in punishment of these offences may be carried into execution upon the approval of the commanding general in the field.

SEC. 22. *And be it further enacted,* That courts-martial shall have power to sentence officers who shall absent themselves from their commands without leave, to be reduced to the ranks to serve three years or during the war.

SEC. 23. *And be it further enacted,* That the clothes, arms, military outfits, and accoutrements furnished by the United States to any soldier shall not be sold, bartered, exchanged, pledged, loaned, or given away; and no person not a soldier, or duly authorized officer of the United States, who has possession of any such clothes, arms, military outfits, or accoutrements, furnished as aforesaid, and which have been the subjects of any such sale, barter, exchange, pledge, loan, or gift, shall have any right, title, or interest therein; but the same may be seized and taken wherever found by any officer of the United States, civil or military, and shall thereupon be delivered to any quartermaster, or other officer authorized to receive the same; and the possession of any such clothes, arms, military outfits, or accoutrements by any person not a soldier or officer of the United States, shall be *prima facie* evidence of such a sale, barter, exchange, pledge, loan, or gift, as aforesaid.

SEC. 24. *And be it further enacted,* That every person not subject to the rules and articles of war who shall procure or entice, or attempt to procure or entice, a soldier in the service of the United States to desert; or who shall harbor, conceal, or give employment to a deserter, or carry him away, or aid in carrying him away, knowing him to be such; or who shall purchase from any soldier his arms, equipments, ammunition, uniform, clothing, or any part thereof; and any captain or commanding officer of any ship or vessel, or any superintendent or conductor of any railroad, or any other public conveyance, carrying away any such soldier as one of his crew or otherwise, knowing him to have deserted, or shall refuse to deliver him up to the orders of his commanding officer, shall, upon legal conviction, be fined, at the discretion of any court having cognizance of the same, in any sum not exceeding five hundred dollars, and he shall be imprisoned not exceeding two years nor less than six months.

SEC. 25. *And be it further enacted,* That if any person shall resist any draft of men enrolled under this act into the service of the United States, or shall counsel or aid any person to resist any such draft; or shall assault or obstruct any officer in making such draft, or in the performance of any service in relation thereto; or shall counsel any person to assault or obstruct any such officer, or shall counsel any drafted men not to appear at the place of rendezvous, or wilfully dissuade them from the performance of military duty as required by law, such person shall be subject to summary arrest by the provost marshal, and shall be forthwith delivered to the civil authorities, and, upon conviction thereof, be punished by a fine not exceeding five hundred dollars, or by imprisonment not exceeding two years, or by both of said punishments.

SEC. 26. *And be it further enacted,* That, immediately after the passage of this act, the President shall issue his proclamation declaring that all soldiers now absent from their regiments without leave may return within a time specified to such place or places as he may indicate in his proclamation, and be restored to their respective regiments without punishment, except the forfeiture of their pay and allowances during their absence; and all deserters who shall not return within the time so specified by the President shall, upon being arrested, be punished as the law provides.

SEC. 27. *And be it further enacted,* That depositions of witnesses residing beyond the limits of the State, Territory or district in which military courts shall be ordered to sit, may be taken in cases not capital by either party, and read in evidence; provided the same shall be taken upon reasonable notice to the opposite party, and duly authenticated.

SEC. 28. *And be it further enacted,* That the judge advocate shall have power to appoint a reporter, whose duty it shall be to record the proceedings of and testimony taken before military courts instead of the judge advocate; and such reporter may take down such proceedings and testimony in the first instance in shorthand. The reporter shall be sworn or affirmed faithfully to perform his duty before entering upon it.

SEC. 29. *And be it further enacted,* That the court shall, for reasonable cause, grant a continuance to either party for such time and as often as shall appear to be just: *Provided,* That if the prisoner be in close confinement, the trial shall not be delayed for a period longer than sixty days.

SEC. 30. *And be it further enacted,* That in time of war, insurrection, or rebellion, murder, assault and battery with an intent to kill, manslaughter, mayhem, wounding by shooting or stabbing with an intent to commit murder, robbery, arson, burglary, rape, assault and battery with an intent to commit rape and larceny, shall be punishable by the sentence of a general court-martial or military commission, when committed by persons who are in the military service of the United States, and subject to the articles of war; and the punishments for such offences shall never be less than those inflicted by the laws of the State, Territory or district in which they may have been committed.

SEC. 31. *And be it further enacted,* That any officer absent from duty with leave, except for sickness or wounds, shall, during his absence, receive half of the pay and allowances prescribed by law, and no more; and any officer absent without leave shall, in addition to the penalties prescribed by law or a court-martial, forfeit all pay or allowances during such absence.

SEC. 32. *And be it further enacted,* That the commanders of regiments and of batteries in the field are hereby authorized and empowered to grant furloughs for a period not exceeding thirty days at any one time to five per centum of the non-commissioned officers and privates, for good conduct in the line of duty and subject to the approval of the commander of the forces of which such non-commissioned officers and privates form a part.

SEC. 33. *And be it further enacted,* That the President of the United States is hereby authorized and empowered, during the present rebellion, to call forth the national forces, by draft, in the manner provided for in this act.

SEC. 34. *And be it further enacted,* That all persons drafted under the provisions of this act shall be assigned by the President to military duty in such corps, regiments, or other branches of the service as the exigencies of the service may require.

SEC. 35. *And be it further enacted,* That hereafter details to special service shall only be made with the consent of the commanding officer of forces in the field; and enlisted men, now or hereafter detailed to special service, shall not receive any extra pay for such services beyond that allowed to other enlisted men.

SEC. 36. *And be it further enacted,* That general orders of the War Department, numbered one hundred and fifty-four and one hundred and sixty-two, in reference to enlistments from the volunteers into the regular service, be, and the same are hereby, rescinded; and hereafter no such enlistments shall be allowed.

SEC. 37. *And be it further enacted*, That the grades created in the cavalry forces of the United States by section eleven of the act approved seventeenth July, eighteen hundred and sixty-two, and for which no rate of compensation has been provided, shall be paid as follows, to wit: Regimental commissary the same as regimental quartermaster; chief trumpeter the same as chief bugler; saddler sergeant the same as regimental commissary sergeant; company commissary sergeant the same as company quartermaster's sergeant: *Provided*, That the grade of supernumerary second lieutenant, and two teamsters for each company, and one chief farrier and blacksmith for each regiment, as allowed by said section of that act, be, and they are hereby, abolished; and each cavalry company may have two trumpeters, to be paid as buglers; and each regiment shall have one veterinary surgeon, with the rank of a regimental sergeant major, whose compensation shall be seventy-five dollars per month.

SEC. 38. *And be it further enacted*, That all persons who, in time of war or of rebellion against the supreme authority of the United States, shall be found lurking or acting as spies in or about any of the fortifications, posts, quarters, or encampments of any of the armies of the United States, or elsewhere, shall be triable by a general court-martial or military commission, and shall, upon conviction, suffer death.

GALUSHA A. GROW,
*Speaker of the House of Representatives.*
SOLOMON FOOT,
*President of the Senate pro tempore.*

Approved March 3, 1863.

ABRAHAM LINCOLN,
*President of the United States.*

www.ingramcontent.com/pod-product-compliance
Lightning Source LLC
Chambersburg PA
CBHW032344020726
47499CB00009B/3167

* 9 7 8 3 3 3 7 3 8 1 0 0 4 *